TRAINSPOTTING
&
SHALLOW GRAVE

TRAINSPOTTING
&
SHALLOW GRAVE

John Hodge

faber and faber
LONDON · BOSTON

First published in 1996
by Faber and Faber Limited
3 Queen Square London WCIN 3AU

Photoset by Parker Typesetting Service, Leicester
Printed in England by Clays Ltd, St Ives plc

A CIP record for this book
is available from the British Library

ISBN 0–571–17968–1

2 4 6 8 10 9 7 5 3

CONTENTS

INTRODUCTION

PART ONE: THE EARLY YEARS

I began writing *Shallow Grave* in the spring of 1991. If I had known then what I know now about the coalition of fortune and favour that must occur before a script becomes a film, I would not have bothered. I knew nothing and no one. I naïvely assumed that all I had to do was write what I liked and all the necessary people would fall into place. They would take the script from my hands and turn it into the film I wanted to see. That this is more or less exactly what happened is a tribute to the beneficial effects of ignorance.

I had this idea about three people in a flat and a stranger and a bag of money and that seemed to me like a film, so I began writing. With a view to an end-of-career auction, the first draft of *Shallow Grave* was hand-written on table napkins, backs of envelopes, etc. I showed it to my sister who introduced me to a guy called Andrew Macdonald who said that he was a 'producer'. This was a lie. He told me that he had worked in Hollywood as a script editor. This was a lie. He told me that he had met Bridget Fonda; that he knew Bridget Fonda well, and implied, more or less, that he had enjoyed a tabloid celebrity-style on-off relationship with Bridget Fonda for several years and that it was only a matter of time before I saw her on the cover of *Hello!* magazine under the headline 'Coping without Andrew: Bridget Fonda's Inner Strength'. He assured me that she would star in our film, along with Ray Liotta and Bill Murray (the two male leads I had in mind). Need I say that this was all one big lie?

I soon discovered the true nature of Macdonald's work 'in television' when I visited the set of *Taggart* and was witness to the spectacle of Bridget Fonda's on-off lover replenishing the store of Andrex in the extras' toilets and then spooning tuna to the leading lady's cat.

But Macdonald and I established a healthy working relationship. I would write a new draft of the script which he would then read and then return with a tactful critique like, 'The second half isn't up to much.' Holding back the tears, I would review the section in question and, to my regular irritation, find myself in agreement. I then indulged in orgies of bloodletting, striking out subplots, characters, and locations, and a couple of months later we would do it all over again.

After about a year and half of this we found ourselves in the offices of Channel Four facing two responsible adults who liked the script but wanted to know just who did we think we were. I would have immediately confessed to our status as bona fide no-hopers but Macdonald intervened and revealed why he is a producer and I am not. I sat in awed silence while he calmly described his background in 'film' and 'television': the formative experiences at Pinewood and Shepperton (back in the days when there was British film industry, of course), the Hollywood years, the loss of faith in the studio system, the return to small-scale, low-budget short film-making, the directorial dabbling, and the limitless commercial and artistic vision. The only thing he missed out was the on-off love affair with Bridget Fonda. It was a marvellous performance. We were instructed to return with a new draft, a budget, and a director.

So while I sweated out another new draft, Macdonald spent the next two months having lunch, which is apparently the accepted method of finding a director.

Danny Boyle was not what I expected. Where were the jodhpurs, the beret, and the megaphone? In conversation he came across as a man of sensitivity and endless patience but with a thuggish streak and a certain low, animal cunning: in short, a man who could work with actors. Any doubts I might have harboured were blown away on our first return to the responsible adults, when Boyle answered the question of how he would direct the film by saying that it would be 'witty, but not expressionist'. I have often pondered on the meaning of this phrase, wondering whether or not it would be altered by rearranging the words.

A few more rewrites were undertaken as the summer drifted by and filming drew ever nearer. My involvement gradually faded out until I reached the role of constitutional monarch, consulted on everything on the understanding that the answer would be 'yes'. This is the writer's lot: anyone who doesn't like it should learn either to lie or to work with actors. I began to plan my retirement.

In February 1994, a few months after the shooting of *Shallow Grave* had finished, Macdonald visited me in my south-coast rest home where he gave me a copy of *Trainspotting* by Irvine Welsh and suggested I read it with a view to screen adaptation. I took the book, read it, and, suitably stunned, I handed it back. *Trainspotting* is an incredible book: its characters, language, narratives, and tone of aggressive entertainment were like nothing I had seen before.

I explained to Macdonald why *Trainspotting* would never make a film.

1) It is a collection of loosely related short stories about several different characters. Only towards the end does it take on a continuous narrative form.

2) The characters, each with a distinctive voice, are defined by internal monologue as much as anything, and the language is uncompromizingly specific to a time and place.

In addition, I pointed out that I had retired from screenwriting.

But Macdonald persisted, implying in a strictly off the record, noncommittal way that my fee might be larger this time. Furthermore, he observed, with perhaps half a century of life ahead of me this charming rest home with its view across to France on a clear day could soon be beyond my means. Thus enslaved again in the degrading business of film, I reread *Trainspotting*. I enjoyed it even more, noticing depth and humanity that I had missed the first time around, having been dazzled then by the language and the horror. But still I didn't see it as a film. Boyle and Macdonald, not being screenwriters (unlike me with my one credit to prove it), were not put off by my protest about the practical difficulties. Their confidence was touching and their suggestions were many even if, at times, they fell short of actually being helpful. Months went by, then some more months, and still they nagged on. I agreed to a two-week brain-storming session to hammer it out once and for all, expecting that either this would be the end of it, or that late at night over takeaway pizza and cold coffee (American cop show fantasy time again) one of us would stand back from the shaving mirror and say: 'I've got it.'

Unfortunately this was not the end of it and there was no takeaway pizza. I went home at five o'clock every day after several hours of discussion on the relative merits of 'sex with the deceased brother's pregnant widow' versus 'fishing through strangers' excrement for the lost morphine suppositories'. Tough one, that.

At the end of this fortnight, Boyle and Macdonald, now quite exhausted by all that thinking but happy that they had given their all to the scripting process, retired to lie in darkened rooms and await the soft plop of script through letterbox.

I read the book again and started writing. My intention was to produce a screenplay which would seem to have, approximately, a beginning, a middle, and an end, would last ninety minutes, and would convey at least some of the spirit and content of the book. This involved amalgamating various characters, transferring incident and dialogue from one character to another, building some scenes around minor details from the book and making up a few things altogether.

If I missed out your favourite bits, well I'm sorry but I missed out some of my own as well. 'Memories of Matty', for example, is probably my favourite chapter: it has enough material for a whole film in itself, but too much to fit into a single scene in this version. All that survives from it is Spud's attention to Australian pop culture after Tommy's funeral, but even that moment is left unexplained in the forward rush of screen time. For a more complete understanding of that scene and all others, please refer to the book.

My own contributions to the script make up a small proportion of it and are not crucial. I am proud, however, to have found a fitting monument at last for Archie Gemmill's goal against Holland in 1978. A whole nation of gullible males was moved by feelings of disappointment, betrayal, and ecstasy during that summer. Seventeen years later it seemed an ideal emotional cocktail for Mark Renton.

It should be stated that throughout this process Irvine Welsh was a saintly model of non-intervention while a complete stranger took liberties with his text. I cannot imagine many authors being so relaxed, especially when the work in question has been recognized as a classic and has found such devotion in the minds of its readers.

I would like to thank the people who helped to construct both these scripts and specifically the following who have all contributed criticism at one time or another: Grace Hodge, Andrew Macdonald, Danny Boyle, David Aukin, Jack Lechner, Allon Reich, Allan Shiach, Chris Young, Marc Berlin, and Walter Donohue. And finally, thank you, Mother and Father, for all the encouragement and support that you have given.

John Hodge
November 1995

Andrew Macdonald, John Hodge and Danny Boyle on location for *Trainspotting*.

Trainspotting

EXT. STREET. DAY

Legs run along the pavement. They are Mark Renton's.

Just ahead of him is Spud. They are both belting along.

As they travel, various objects (pens, tapes, CDs, toiletries, ties, sunglasses, etc.) either fall or are discarded from inside their jackets.

They are pursued by two hard-looking Store Detectives in identical uniforms. The men are fast, but Renton and Spud maintain their lead.

> RENTON
> (*voice-over*)

Choose life. Choose a job. Choose a career. Choose a family. Choose a fucking big television, choose washing machines, cars, compact disc players and electrical tin openers.

Suddenly, as Renton crosses a road, a car skids to a halt, inches from him.

In a moment of detachment he stops and looks at the shocked driver, then at Spud, who has continued running, then at the Two Men, who are now closing on him.

He smiles.

INT. SWANNEY'S FLAT ROOM. DAY

In a bare, dingy room, Renton lies on the floor, alone, motionless and drugged.

> RENTON
> (*voice-over*)

Choose good health, low cholesterol and dental insurance. Choose fixed-interest mortgage repayments. Choose a starter home. Choose your friends.

On a floodlit five-a-side pitch, Renton and his friends are taking on another team at football.

The opposition all wear an identical strip (Arsenal), whereas Renton and his friends wear an odd assortment of gear.

Three girls – Lizzy, Gail and Allison and Baby – stand by the side, watching.

The boys are outclassed by the team with the strip but play much dirtier.

As each performs a characteristic bit of play, the play freezes and their name is visible, printed or written on some item of clothing (T-shirt, baseball cap, shorts, trainers). In Begbie's case, his name appears as a tattoo on his arm.

Sick Boy commits a sneaky foul and indignantly denies it.

Begbie commits an obvious foul and makes no effort to deny it.

Spud, in goal, lets the ball in between his legs.

Tommy kicks the ball as hard as he can.

Renton's litany continues over the action:

RENTON
(voice-over)

Choose leisurewear and matching luggage. Choose a three-piece suite on hire purchase in a range of fucking fabrics. Choose DIY and wondering who the fuck you are on a Sunday morning. Choose sitting on that couch watching mind-numbing, spirit-crushing game shows, stuffing fucking junk food into your mouth. Choose rotting away at the end of it all, pishing your last in a miserable home, nothing more than an embarrassment to the selfish, fucked-up brats you have spawned to replace yourself. Choose your future. Choose life.

Renton is hit straight in the face by the ball. He lies back on the astroturf. Voice-over continues.

But why would I want to do a thing like that?

INT. SWANNEY'S FLAT. DAY

Renton lies on the floor.

Swanney, Allison and Baby, Sick Boy and Spud are shooting up or preparing to shoot up. Sick Boy is talking to Allison as he taps up a vein on her arm.

> RENTON
> (*voice-over*)

I chose not to choose life: I chose something else. And the reasons? There are no reasons. Who needs reasons when you've got heroin?

> SICK BOY

Goldfinger's better than *Dr No*. Both of them are a lot better than *Diamonds are Forever*, a judgement reflected in its relative poor showing at the box office, in which field, of course, *Thunderball* was a notable success.

> RENTON
> (*voice-over*)

People think it's all about misery and desperation and death and all that shite, which is not to be ignored, but what they forget –

> *Spud is shooting up.*

is the pleasure of it. Otherwise we wouldn't do it. After all, we're not fucking stupid. At least, we're not that fucking stupid. Take the best orgasm you ever had, multiply it by a thousand and you're still nowhere near it. When you're on junk you have only one worry: scoring. When you're off it you are suddenly obliged to worry about all sorts of other shite. Got no money: can't get pished. Got money: drinking too much. Can't get a bird: no chance of a ride. Got a bird: too much hassle. You have to worry about bills, about food, about some football team that never fucking wins, about human relationships and all the things that really don't matter when you've got a sincere and truthful junk habit.

> SICK BOY

I would say, in those days, he was a muscular actor, in every sense, with all the presence of someone like Cooper or Lancaster, but

5

combined with a sly wit to make him a formidable romantic lead, closer in that respect to Cary Grant.

> RENTON
> (*voice-over*)

The only drawback, or at least the principal drawback, is that you have to endure all manner of cunts telling you that –

INT. PUB I. NIGHT

Begbie, smoking and drinking, speaks to camera.

> BEGBIE

No way would I poison my body with that shite, all they fucking chemicals, no fucking way.

INT. PUB I. NIGHT

Tommy sits beside Lizzy. He speaks to camera.

> TOMMY

It's a waste of your life, Rents, poisoning your body with that shite.

INT. RENTON FAMILY HOME, LIVING ROOM. NIGHT

Renton's father and mother sit at the table eating.

Renton is seated but not eating.

> FATHER

Every chance you've ever had, you've blown it, stuffing your veins with that filth.

*[INT. ELECTRICAL RETAILERS. DAY

Gav wears the corporate jacket.

> GAV

Get off that stuff, Rents, and get a job. It's not as bad as it looks. While you're here, you don't fancy buying a cooker, do you?]

*Cut from completed film.

INT. SWANNEY'S FLAT. DAY

Sick Boy and Spud lie drugged up. Allison and Baby wait while Swanney cooks up.

Renton is standing up.

> RENTON
> (*voice-over*)
> From time to time, even I have uttered the magic words.

> SWANNEY
> Are you serious?

> RENTON
> Yeah. No more. I'm finished with that shite.

> SWANNEY
> Well, it's up to you.

> RENTON
> I'm going to get it right this time. Going to get it set up and get off it for good.

> SWANNEY
> Sure, sure. I've heard it before.

> RENTON
> The Sick Boy method.

They both look at Sick Boy.

> SWANNEY
> Yeah, well, it surely worked for him.

> RENTON
> He's always been lacking in moral fibre.

> SWANNEY
> He knows a lot about Sean Connery.

> RENTON
> That's hardly a substitute.

> SWANNEY
> You'll need one more hit.

RENTON

No, I don't think so.

SWANNEY

To see you through the night that lies ahead.

Freeze frame on Swanney.

RENTON
(*voice-over*)

We called him the mother superior on account of the length of his habit. He knew all about it. On it, off it, he knew it all. Of course I'd have another shot: after all, I had work to do.

INT. RENTON'S FLAT ROOM. DAY

The door opens and Renton enters carrying shopping bags. He empties them on to a mattress beside three buckets and a television.

RENTON
(*voice-over*)

Relinquishing junk. Stage One: preparation. For this you will need: one room which you will not leave; one mattress; tomato soup, ten tins of; mushroom soup, eight tins of, for consumption cold; ice cream, vanilla, one large tub of; Magnesia, Milk of, one bottle; paracetamol; mouth wash; vitamins; mineral water; Lucozade; pornography; one bucket for urine, one for faeces, and one for vomitus; one television; and one bottle of Valium, which I have already procured, from my mother, who is, in her own domestic and socially aceptable way, also a drug addict.

Renton swallows several Valium tablets. Voice-over continues.

And now I'm ready. All I need is a final hit to soothe the pain while the Valium takes effect.

*[INT. SWANNEY'S FLAT. DAY

Swanney, Sick Boy, Spud and Allison and Baby all lie inert while the telephone rings.]

*Cut from completed film.

9

INT. CALL BOX. DAY

Renton curses as he slams down the receiver. He dials again.

>   RENTON
> Mikey. It's Mark Renton. Can you help me out?

INT. MIKEY'S FLAT. DAY

Renton holds two opium suppositories in the palm of his hand.

>   RENTON
>   (*voice-over*)
> This was typical of Mikey Forrester.
>   (*on screen*)
> What the fuck are these?
>   (*voice-over*)
> Under the normal run of things I would have had nothing to do
> with the cunt, but this was not the normal run of things.

>   MIKEY
> Opium suppositories. Ideal for your purpose. Slow release, like.
> Bring you down gradually. Custom fucking designed for your
> needs.

>   RENTON
> I want a fucking hit.

>   MIKEY
> That's all I've got: take it or leave it.

Renton sticks his hand down the back of his trousers and sticks the suppositories into his rectum.

Feel better now?

>   RENTON
> For all the good they've done me I might as well have stuck them
> up my arse.

He smiles.

II

EXT. STREET. DAY

> RENTON
> (*voice-over*)

Heroin makes you constipated. The heroin from my last hit is fading away and the suppositories have yet to melt. I am no longer constipated.

He looks around the local amenities. He is in discomfort, clutching his abdomen and falling to his knees.

He notices a betting shop.

INT. BETTING SHOP. DAY

Renton walks through the crowded, smoky betting shop towards a door market 'toilet' with a bit of card.

> RENTON
> (*voice-over*)

I fantasize about a massive pristine convenience.

He stumbles through.

> (*voice-over*)

Brilliant gold taps, virginal white marble, a seat carved from ebony, a cistern full of Chanel No. 5, and a flunky handing me pieces of raw silk toilet roll. But under the circumstances I'll settle for anywhere.

INT. HORRIBLE TOILET. DAY

This is the most horrible toilet in Britain.

Alone, Renton makes his way through the horrors to a cubicle.

INT. HORRIBLE TOILET CUBICLE. DAY

Renton locks the door.

He looks into the bowl and winces with disgust, even in his state.

He pulls the chain. The chain comes off.

He drops his trousers, sits on the bowl and closes his eyes.

*[MONTAGE

A lorry on a buliding site dumps a load of bricks, B52s shed their load on Vietnam, the Blue Peter *elephant, etc.*]

INT. CUBICLE. DAY

Renton has his eyes closed. They snap open.

He looks down between his legs.

He drops to his knees in front of the bowl and rolls his sleeve up.

With no more hesitation he plunges his arm into the bowl and trawls for the suppositories.

It seems to take ages. He cannot find them. He sticks his arm further and further into the toilet, moving his whole body closer. He strains to find it.

His head is over the bowl now. Gradually he reaches still further until his head is lowered into the bowl, followed by his neck, torso, other arm, and finally his legs, all disappearing.

The cubicle is empty.

INT. UNDER WATER. DAY

Renton, dressed as before, swims through murky depths until he reaches the bottom, where he picks up the suppositories, which glow like luminous pearls, before heading up towards the surface again.

INT. HORRIBLE TOILET CUBICLE. DAY

The toilet is empty.

Suddenly Renton appears through the bowl, then his arms as he lifts himself out. Still clasping his two suppositories, he walks out of the toilet.

INT. RENTON'S ROOM. DAY

The mattress, buckets and supplies are laid out as before.

The door opens and Renton enters, still soaking and dripping.

*Cut from completed film.

13

The suppositories are in his hand. He holds them up, and they twinkle in the light.

RENTON

Now. Now I'm ready.

INT. RENTON'S ROOM. DAY

The cans of soup, the bottle of water and the carton of ice cream are empty, the bottles of pills spilt, the magazines well thumbed.

*[SICK BOY

You Only Live Twice?

RENTON

Nineteen-sixty-seven.

SICK BOY

Running time?

RENTON

One hundred and sixteen minutes.

SICK BOY

Director?

RENTON

Lewis Gilbert.

SICK BOY

Screenwriter?

RENTON

Eh – Ian Fleming?

SICK BOY

Fuck off! He never wrote any of them.

RENTON

OK, so who was it, then?

SICK BOY

You can look it up.

*Cut from completed film.

Sick Boy throws across a worn copy of a film guide. Renton cannot be bothered to pick it up.

How are you feeling since you came off the skag? For myself, I'm bored.

RENTON

Who wrote it?

SICK BOY

But you're looking better, it has to be said. Healthier. Radiant even.

RENTON

You don't know, do you?

SICK BOY

And I wondered if you'd care to go to the park tomorrow.

RENTON

The park?

SICK BOY

Tomorrow afternoon. Usual set-up.

RENTON

Who wrote it?

SICK BOY

Roald Dahl.

RENTON

Roald Dahl. Fuck me.]

EXT. PARK. DAY

Typical weather, neither good nor bad. The park is nondescript arid green with a few bushes. This is not Kew Gardens. Renton and Sick Boy appear, dressed as before but for the addition of cheap sunglasses.

Renton is carrying a battered old cassette player and a carry-out in a plastic bag.

Sick Boy is carrying a small, tatty suitcase from Oxfam.

They scan the horizon and give each other the nod. They walk towards the bushes.

RENTON
(*voice-over*)

The downside of coming off junk was that I knew I would need to mix with my friends again in a state of full consciousness. It was awful: they reminded me so much of myself I could hardly bear to look at them. Take Sick Boy, for instance, he came off junk at the same time as me, not because he wanted to, you understand, but just to annoy me, just to show me how easily he could do it, thereby downgrading my own struggle. Sneaky fucker, don't you think? And when all I wanted to do was lie alone and feel sorry for myself, he insisted on telling me once again about his unifying theory of life.

EXT. PARK. DAY

Seen through the telescopic sight of an air rifle that wanders over various potential targets (children, pensioners, couples, gardeners, etc.).

SICK BOY

It's certainly a phenomenon in all walks of life.

RENTON

What do you mean?

SICK BOY

Well, at one time, you've got it, and then you lose it, and it's gone for ever. All walks of life: George Best, for example, had it and lost it, or David Bowie, or Lou Reed –

RENTON

Some of his solo stuff's not bad.

SICK BOY

No, it's not bad, but it's not great either, is it? And in your heart you kind of know that although it sounds all right, it's actually just shite.

RENTON

So who else?

SICK BOY

Charlie Nicholas, David Niven, Malcolm McLaren, Elvis Presley –

RENTON

OK, OK, so what's the point you're trying to make?

EXT. PARK. DAY

Sick Boy rests the gun down.

SICK BOY

All I'm trying to do is help you understand that *The Name of the Rose* is merely a blip on an otherwise uninterrupted downward trajectory.

RENTON

What about *The Untouchables*?

SICK BOY

I don't rate that at all.

RENTON

Despite the Academy award?

SICK BOY

That means fuck all. The sympathy vote.

RENTON

Right. So we all get old and then we can't hack it any more. Is that it?

SICK BOY

Yeah.

RENTON

That's your theory?

SICK BOY

Yeah. Beautifully fucking illustrated.

RENTON

Give me the gun.

EXT. PARK. DAY

Through the sight again. This time a Skinhead and his muscle-bound dog are in view.

Sick Boy and Renton talk like Sean Connery.

SICK BOY

Do you see the beast? Have you got it in your sights?

RENTON

Clear enough, Moneypenny. This should present no significant problem.

> *The gun fires and the dog yelps, jumps up and bites its owner (the Skinhead).*

SICK BOY

For a vegetarian, Rents, you're a fucking evil shot.

EXT. PARK. DAY

Renton loads up again.

RENTON
(*voice-over*)

Without heroin, I attempted to lead a useful and fulfilling life as a good citizen.

INT. CAFÉ. DAY

Two milkshakes clink together.

Renton and Spud are seated at a booth, dressed in their own fashion for job interviews.

RENTON

Good luck, Spud.

SPUD

Cheers.

RENTON

Now remember –

SPUD

Yeah.

RENTON

If they think you're not trying, you're in trouble. First hint of that, they'll be on to the DSS, 'This cunt's no trying' and your Giro is fucking finished, right?

SPUD

Right.

RENTON

But try too hard –

SPUD

And you might get the fucking job.

RENTON

Exactly.

SPUD

Nightmare.

RENTON

It's a tightrope, Spud, a fucking tightrope.

SPUD

My problem is that I tend to clam up. I go dumb and I can't answer any questions at all. Nerves on the big occasion, like a footballer.

RENTON

Try this.

Renton unfolds silver foil to reveal some amphetamine. Spud dips in a finger and takes a dab. He nods in appreciation as he tastes it. Renton leaves the packet in Spud's hand.

SPUD

A little dab of speed is just the ticket.

*[INT. INTERVIEW OFFICE. DAY

A Woman and Two Men (1 and 2) are interviewing Renton. His job application form is on the desk in front of them.

MAN 1

Well, Mr Renton, I see that you attended the Royal Edinburgh College.

RENTON

Indeed, yes, those halcyon days.

*Cut from completed film.

MAN I

One of Edinburgh's finest schools.

RENTON

Oh, yes, indeed. I look back on my time there with great fondness and affection. The debating society, the first eleven, the soft knock of willow on leather –

MAN I

I'm an old boy myself, you know?

RENTON

Oh, really?

MAN I

Do you recall the school motto?

RENTON

Of course, the motto, the motto –

MAN I

Strive, hope, believe and conquer.

RENTON

Exactly. Those very words have been my guiding light in what is, after all, a dark and often hostile world.

Renton looks pious under scrutiny.

MAN 2

Mr Renton –

RENTON

Yes.

MAN 2

You seem eminently suited to this post but I wonder if you could explain the gaps in your employment record?

RENTON

Yes, I can. The truth – well, the truth is that I've had a long-standing problem with heroin addiction. I've been known to sniff it, smoke it, swallow it, stick it up my arse and inject it into my veins. I've been trying to combat this addiction, but unless you count social security scams and shoplifting, I haven't had a regular

21

job in years. I feel it's important to mention this.

There is silence.

A paper clip crashes to the floor.]

INT. OFFICE. DAY

The same office. The same team are interviewing Spud.

SPUD

No, actually I went to Craignewton but I was worried that you wouldn't have heard of it so I put the Royal Edinburgh College instead, because they're both schools, right, and we're all in this together, and I wanted to put across the general idea rather than the details, yeah? People get all hung up on details, but what's the point? Like which school? Does it matter? Why? When? Where? Or how many O grades did I get? Could be six, could be one, but that's not important. What's important is that I am, right? That I am.

MAN I

Mr Murphy, do you mean that you lied on your application?

SPUD

Only to get my foot in the door. Showing initiative, right?

MAN I

You were referred here by the Department of Employment. There's no need for you to get your 'foot in the door', as you put it.

SPUD

Hey. Right. No problem. Whatever you say, man. You're the man, the governor, the dude in the chair, like. I'm merely here. But obviously I am. Here, that is. I hope I'm not talking too much. I don't usually. I think it's all important though, isn't it?

MAN 2

Mr Murphy, what attracts you to the leisure industry?

SPUD

In a word, pleasure. My pleasure in other people's leisure.

*[
WOMAN

What do you see as your main strengths?

SPUD

I love people. All people. Even people that no one else loves, I think they're OK, you know. Like Beggars.

WOMAN

Homeless people?

SPUD

No, not homeless people. Beggars, Francis Begbie – one of my mates. I wouldn't say my best mate, I mean, sometimes the boy goes over the score, like one time when we – me and him – were having a laugh and all of a sudden he's fucking gubbed me in the face, right –]

WOMAN

Mr Murphy, *[leaving your friend aside,] do you see yourself as having any weaknesses?

SPUD

I have to admit it: I'm a perfectionist. For me, it's the best or nothing at all. If things go badly, I can't be bothered, but I have a good feeling about this interview. Seems to me like it's gone pretty well. We've touched on a lot of subjects, a lot of things to think about, for all of us.

MAN I

Thank you, Mr Murphy. We'll let you know.

SPUD

The pleasure was mine. Best interview I've ever been to. Thanks.

Spud crosses the room to shake everyone by the hand and kiss them.

RENTON
(voice-over)

Spud had done well. I was proud of him. He fucked up good and proper.

*Cut from completed film.

23

[INT. PUB I. DAY

Renton and Spud meet up after the interviews.

                    SPUD
A little too well, if anything, a little too well, that's my only fear,
compadre.

                    RENTON
Another dab?

                    SPUD
Would not say no, would not say no.

INT. OFFICE. DAY

The Woman and Two Men sit in silence.]

INT. PUB 2. NIGHT

*It is Saturday night in a busy, city-centre pub on two levels. On a large
upper balcony, overlooking the bar and floor downstairs, sit Spud, Gail,
Renton, Sick Boy, Tommy, Lizzy and Begbie.*

Begbie's story overlaps with the subsequent depiction of the incident.

                    BEGBIE
                 (*voice-over*)
Picture the scene. Wednesday morning in the Volley. Me and
Tommy are playing pool. No problems, and I'm playing like Paul
fucking Newman by the way. I'm giving the boy here the tanning of a
lifetime. So anyway, it comes to the final ball, the deciding shot of the
tournament: I'm on the black and he's sitting in the corner, looking
all biscuit-arsed. Then this hard cunt comes in. Obviously fancied
himself. Starts looking at me. Right fucking at me. Trying to put off,
like, just for kicks. Looking at me as if to say, 'Come ahead, square
go.' Well, you know me, I'm no looking for trouble but at the end of
the day I'm the cunt with the pool cue and I'm game for a swedge. So
I squared up, casual like. So what does the hard cunt do, or so-called
hard cunt? Shites it. Puts down his drink, turns around and gets the
fuck out of there. And after that, the game was mine.

*Cut from completed film.

24

INT. POOL HALL. DAY

The events in the pool hall, as described by Begbie.

Begbie and Tommy are playing pool.

Begbie is playing like a wizard.

Tommy looks defeated.

Lining up for the final ball, Begbie is distracted by a large Hard Man standing at the bar staring at him.

Begbie stands up and walks slowly towards the Hard Man.

They stand, eye to eye, for a moment.

Begbie swings the pool cue slowly into his palm.

The Hard Man turns and leaves.

Begbie drinks the Hard Man's pint, then pots the black with a brilliant shot.

INT. PUB 2. DAY

Begbie, his story complete, finishes his pint. The others continue to stare at him, frozen as though expecting something more. Begbie smiles and throws the pint glass over his head.

Freeze-frame: the glass in mid-air and Begbie's smiling face.

RENTON
(*voice-over*)

And that was it. That was Begbie's story. Or at least that was Begbie's version of the story. But a couple of days later I got the truth from Tommy. It was one of his major weaknesses: he never told lies, never took drugs, and never cheated on anyone.

INT. TOMMY'S FLAT. DAY

Renton's hand flicks through a long row of videos on the floor while the sound of weights being lifted (by Tommy) emanates from nearby.

Most of the videos are feature films or comedy shows, some with titles written in Tommy's hand, but two catch Renton's attention.

They are 100 Great Goals *and* Tommy and Lizzy, Vol. 1, *the latter a handwritten title.*

Renton looks from the videos round to Tommy, who is engrossed in lifting weights.

TOMMY

Well, sure it was Wednesday morning, we were in the Volley playing pool, that much is true.

INT. POOL HALL. DAY

Tommy's account over a depiction of his version.

TOMMY
(*voice-over*)

But Begbie is playing absolutely fucking gash. He's got a hangover so bad he can hardly hold the fucking cue, never mind pot the ball. I'm doing my best to lose, trying to humour him, like, but it's not doing any good: every time I touch the ball I pot something, every time Begbie goes near the table he fucks it up. So he's got the hump, right, but finally I manage to set it up so all he's got to do is pot the black to win one game and salvage a little pride and maybe not kick my head in, right. So he's on the black, pressure shot, and it all goes wrong, big time. What does he do? Picks on this specky wee gadge at the bar and accuses him of putting him off by looking at him. Can you believe it? I mean, the poor cunt hasn't even glanced in our direction. He's sitting there quiet as a mouse when Beggars gubs him with the cue. He was going to chib him, I tell you, then I thought he was going to do me. The Beggar is fucking psycho, but he's a mate, you know, so what can you do?

The events are as follows:

Begbie and Tommy are playing pool.

Begbie, furious, miscues, goes in off, etc.

Tommy deliberately misses sitters and tries to look annoyed.

Begbie lines up to play the black. It is unmissable.

At the bar beyond sits a harmless young Man, wearing the same clothes as the Hard Man in Begbie's account except that they are now

26

baggy rather than taut. He is clearly not staring at Begbie but drinks a half-pint and eats some crisps.

As Begbie plays, the Man bites a crisp.

Begbie miscues, rips the cloth and the ball flies off the table.

Tommy catches it and looks up to see Begbie assaulting the young Man.

Tommy cautiously restrains Begbie as he reaches into his jacket for a knife.

Begbie turns and for a moment looks as though he might attack Tommy.

INT. TOMMY'S FLAT. DAY

Tommy puts down his weights.

Renton holds up 100 Great Goals.

> RENTON

Can I borrow this one?

INT. PUB 2. NIGHT

The freeze-frame of the glass in mid-air and Begbie's smiling face.

> RENTON
> (*voice-over*)

Yeah, the guy's a psycho, but it's true, he's a mate as well, so what can you do? Just stand back and watch and try not to get involved. Begbie didn't do drugs either, he just did people. That's what he got off on: his own sensory addiction.

The glass falls into the crowd.

Screaming starts. A Woman is bleeding from a wound in her head. The Men beside her turn furiously around to look for the source of the glass.

Up on the balcony, Begbie stands up. The screams and shouting continue below.

Begbie appears at the bottom of the staircase down from the balcony.

27

He strides towards the bleeding Woman and begins shouting.

BEGBIE

All right. Nobody move. The girl got glassed and no cunt leaves here until we find out which cunt did it.

A Man stands up from one of the tables.

MAN

And who the fuck do you think you are?

Begbie kicks the Man in the groin. Another moves towards him but is blocked by the Men surrounding the girl. Soon the whole mass dissolves into a brutal scrum, in which Begbie plays a prominent part.

Up on the balcony, the rest of the gang watch in silence.

INT. RENTON'S FLAT. DAY

The empty cover for 100 Great Goals *lies on the floor.*

Sick Boy and Renton sit dispassionately watching Tommy and Lizzy in their home-made soft-porn video.

RENTON
(*voice-over*)

And as I sat watching the intimate and highly personal video, stolen only hours earlier from one of my best friends, I realized that something important was missing from my life.

INT. CLUB. NIGHT

A mass of dancing bodies fills the floor. The music is very loud.

At the side of the dance floor sit Tommy and Spud. They look rather gloomy. There is an empty seat beside each of them. Spud is drinking heavily.

Tommy turns and speaks to Spud. His lips move but nothing is audible. Spud is not even aware that Tommy has spoken.

Tommy bellows in Spud's ear.

Tommy's words and all subsequent conversation in the dance area of the

club appear as subtitles, the characters' communications somewhere between speech and mime.

TOMMY

How's it going with Gail?

SPUD

No joy yet.

TOMMY

How long is it?

SPUD

Six weeks.

TOMMY

Six weeks!

SPUD

It's a nightmare. She told me she didn't want our relationship to start on a physical basis as that is how it would be principally defined from then on in.

TOMMY

Where did she come up with that?

SPUD

She read it in *Cosmopolitan*.

TOMMY

Six weeks and no sex?

SPUD

I've got balls like watermelons, I'm telling you.

INT. NIGHTCLUB, WOMEN'S TOILET. NIGHT

Gail and Lizzy are smoking and talking.

GAIL

I read it in *Cosmopolitan*.

LIZZY

It's an interesting theory.

GAIL

Actually it's a nightmare. I've been desperate for a shag, but watching him suffer was just too much fun. You should try it with Tommy.

LIZZY

What, and deny myself the only pleasure I get from him? Did I tell you about my birthday?

GAIL

What happened?

LIZZY

He forgot. Useless motherfucker.

INT. NIGHTCLUB. DANCE AREA. NIGHT

Tommy and Spud seated as before. Their words are subtitled.

As they are speaking Gail and Lizzy return and sit down.

TOMMY

Useless motherfucker, that's what she called me. I told her, I'm sorry, but these things happen. Let's put it behind us.

SPUD

That's fair enough.

30

TOMMY

Yes, but then she finds out I've bought a ticket for Iggy Pop the same night.

SPUD

Went ballistic?

TOMMY

Big time. Absolutely fucking radge. 'It's me or Iggy Pop, time to decide.'

SPUD

So what's it going to be?

TOMMY

Well, I've paid for the ticket.

GAIL and LIZZY

What are you two talking about?

TOMMY and SPUD

Football. What were you talking about?

GAIL and LIZZY

Shopping.

Standing nearby but apart from them is Renton.

Renton notes Spud and Tommy with their partners, and across the other side Sick Boy and Begbie are engaged in flirtatious conversation with Two Women.

RENTON
(*voice-over*)

The situation was becoming serious. Young Renton noticed the haste with which the successful, in the sexual sphere as in all others, segregated themselves from the failures.

Begbie and Sick Boy with the Two Women.

Renton standing among a group of lone nerds.

Renton wades on to the dance floor, looking at countless women, all of whom either turn away or are spoken for.

31

(*voice-over*)

Heroin had robbed Renton of his sex drive, but now it returned with a vengeance. And as the impotence of those days faded into memory, grim desperation took hold in his sex-crazed mind. His post-junk libido, fuelled by alcohol and amphetamine, taunted him remorselessly with his own unsatisfied desire dot dot dot.

Renton notices one girl (Diane) walking on her own towards the door.

A Man carrying two drinks catches up with her and walks backwards, talking to her.

She says nothing. He blocks her way.

She takes one drink and downs it, then the other, handing him back the empty glasses. She steps past him and walks on towards the door.

(*voice-over*)

And with that, Mark Renton had fallen in love.

EXT. STREET. NIGHT

The Girl walks away from the club, scanning the street for a taxi, and hails one which stops just as Renton calls out.

RENTON

Excuse me, I don't mean to harass you, but I was very impressed by the capable and stylish manner in which you dealt with that situation. I thought to myself: she's special.

DIANE

Thanks.

RENTON

What's your name?

DIANE

Diane.

RENTON

Where are you going, Diane?

DIANE

I'm going home.

32

RENTON

Where's that?

DIANE

It's where I live.

RENTON

Great.

DIANE

What?

RENTON

I'll come back if you like, but I'm not promising anything.

Diane halts abruptly as a taxi pulls up.

DIANE

Do you find that this approach usually works, or, let me guess, you've never tried it before. In fact, you don't normally approach girls, am I right? The truth is that you're a quiet, sensitive type but if I'm prepared to take a chance I might just get to know the inner you: witty, adventurous, passionate, loving, loyal, a little bit crazy, a little bit bad, but, hey, don't us girls just love that?

RENTON

Eh –

DIANE

Well, what's wrong, boy? Cat got your tongue?

RENTON

I think I left something back at the –

The girl has disappeared into the back of the taxi.

Renton looks around.

TAXI DRIVER

Are you getting in or not, pal?

EXT. ROAD. NIGHT

The taxi motors along.

INT. TAXI. NIGHT

Renton and Diane are kissing passionately in the back.

EXT. STREET. NIGHT

Spud is pushed against the wall held by his lapels. He drinks from a bottle of beer in one hand.

> GAIL

Do you understand?

Spud nods drunkenly.

Gail releases her grip.

Our relationship is not being redefined; it is developing in an appropriate, organic fashion. I expect you to be a considerate and thoughtful lover, generous but firm. Failure on your part to live up to these very reasonable expectations will result in swift resumption of a non-sex situation. Right?

Spud drinks from a bottle in the other hand and says nothing but does not look too happy.

INT. TOMMY'S FLAT. NIGHT

Tommy and Lizzy kiss while Tommy unlocks the door.

INT. DIANE'S HOME, HALLWAY. NIGHT

In a darkened suburban hallway, the door opens and two figures enter.

> RENTON

Diane.

> DIANE

Ssshh!

> RENTON

Sorry.

> DIANE

Shut up.

They walk through another door and close it behind them.

INT. TOMMY'S FLAT. NIGHT

Tommy and Lizzy kiss against the inside of the door, taking their outer clothes off.

INT. DIANE'S BEDROOM. NIGHT

By a pale bedside light, Diane and Renton undress.

INT. GAIL'S BEDROOM. NIGHT

Spud is lying unconscious on the bed. Gail stands over him.

GAIL

Wake up, Spud, wake up. Sex.

She kicks him. He moans.

Casual sex.

She kicks him again. He moans again.

You useless bastard. So let's see what I'm missing.

She begins undressing him.

INT. DIANE'S BEDROOM. NIGHT

Renton lies on his back while Diane rides above him.

INT. GAIL'S BEDROOM. NIGHT

Gail throws Spud's clothes to the floor and throws a blanket over him.

GAIL

Not much.

She switches out the light.

INT. TOMMY'S FLAT. NIGHT

Tommy and Lizzy now lie on the bed in a state of semi-undress.

LIZZY

Tommy, let's put the tape on.

TOMMY

Now?

LIZZY

Yes, I want to watch ourselves while we're screwing.

TOMMY

Fuck, OK.

Tommy gets up and reaches into the row of videos on the floor. He lifts out Tommy and Lizzy, Vol. 1 *and hastily shoves it into the video.*

Tommy sits back on the bed with the remote control and presses 'play' as Lizzy kisses him.

His face registers consternation.

On the television, Archie Gemmill scores his famous goal against Holland in 1978.

INT. DIANE'S BEDROOM. NIGHT

Renton and Diane climax together.

Diane immediately climbs off and wraps herself in a robe.

RENTON

Christ, I haven't felt that good since Archie Gemmill scored against Holland in 1978.

DIANE

Right. You can't sleep here.

RENTON

What?

DIANE

Out.

RENTON

Come on.

DIANE

No argument. You can sleep on the sofa in the living room, or go home. It's up to you.

RENTON

Jesus.

DIANE

And don't make any noise.

INT. TOMMY'S FLAT. NIGHT

The lights are full on now. Lizzy sits on the bed clutching a blanket around herself.

Tommy hops around in his underwear, searching desperately.

All the videos are opened and scattered everywhere.

LIZZY

What do you mean, it's 'gone'? Where has it gone, Tommy?

TOMMY

It'll be here somewhere. I might have returned it by mistake.

LIZZY

Returned it? Where? To the video shop, Tommy? To the fucking video store? So every punter in Edinburgh is jerking off to our video? God, Tommy, I feel sick.

INT. DIANE'S HOME, LIVING-ROOM. MORNING

Renton lies submerged under a blanket.

The sounds of a normal morning travel from a room nearby: whistles, radio, voices.

Renton peeps over the edge of the blanket, then covers his head again.

INT. GAIL'S BEDROOM. MORNING

Spud opens his eyes. With his fingers, he feels crusted liquid around his mouth.

Abruptly he turns around: the bed is soaked in vomit.

He looks under the cover and drops it again in revulsion.

INT. DIANE'S HOME, LIVING-ROOM. DAY

Renton pulls himself up off the sofa and dresses as quickly as possible.

INT. GAIL'S BEDROOM. DAY

Spud wipes the vomit from his chest with a pillowcase, which he dumps in the middle of the sheets before gathering the whole lot up as a bundle.

INT. DIANE'S HOME, HALL/KITCHEN. DAY

The door swings open. A Man and Woman, about Renton's age, sit at the kitchen table. They look up to see Renton in the doorway.

MAN

Good morning.

WOMAN

Come in and sit down. You must be Mark.

Renton walks to the table and sits down.

RENTON

Yes, that's me.

WOMAN

You're a friend of Diane's?

RENTON

More of a friend of a friend, really.

MAN

Right.

RENTON

Are you her flatmates?

The couple exchange a look and laugh.

WOMAN

Flatmates. I must remember that one.

The Man and Woman look beyond Renton. He too turns and follows their gaze.

Diane stands in the doorway.

She is wearing school uniform.

INT. GAIL'S HOME, HALL/KITCHEN. DAY

The door swings open to reveal the kitchen. Gail, her Father and Mother are seated around the table, eating breakfast.

They look towards Spud, who carries the knotted bundle of sheets as he approaches the table.

> GAIL

Good morning, Spud.

> SPUD

Morning, Gail. Morning, Mrs Houston, Mr Houston.

> MOTHER

Morning, Spud. Sit down and have some breakfast.

> SPUD

Sorry about last night –

> GAIL

It's all right. I slept fine on the sofa.

SPUD

I had a little too much to drink. I'm afraid I had a slight accident.

FATHER

Oh, don't worry, these things happen. It does everyone good to cut loose once in a while.

GAIL

This one could do with being tied up once in a while.

MOTHER

I'll put the sheets in the washing machine just now.

SPUD

No, I'll wash them. I'll take them home and bring them back.

MOTHER

There's no need.

SPUD

It's no problem.

MOTHER

No problem for me either.

She advances to take the bundle. Spud steps back.

SPUD

Really, no.

MOTHER

Honestly, it's no problem.

SPUD

I'd really rather take care of it myself.

MOTHER

Spud, they're my sheets.

She takes hold of the bundle.

Spud does not yield.

She pulls harder. Spud holds on. She tugs powerfully.

The bundle bursts open with an explosion of vomit and excrement

41

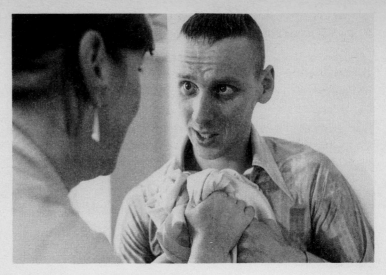

that covers everything in the kitchen.

Only Spud remains untouched.

*[SPUD
I guess this means I'll never get to have sex with Gail.

INT. TOMMY'S FLAT. DAY

Tommy sits alone, watching 100 Great Goals.]

EXT. STREET. DAY

Renton paces briskly down the street, followed by Diane.

DIANE
I don't see why not.

RENTON
Because it's illegal.

DIANE
Holding hands?

*Cut from completed film.

RENTON

No, not holding hands.

DIANE

In that case you can do it. You were quite happy to do a lot more last night.

RENTON

And that's what's illegal. Do you know what they do to people like me inside? They'd cut my balls off and flush them down the fucking toilet.

They stop at the school gates.

DIANE

Calm down. You're not going to jail.

RENTON

Easy for you to say.

DIANE

Can I see you again?

RENTON

Certainly not.

Renton walks away.

DIANE

If you don't see me again I'll tell the police.

Renton turns and walks back to her. They stand for a moment, then Renton walks away again. Diane smiles.

(*to herself*)

I'll see you around then.

EXT. VIDEO STORE. DAY

In the cold light of morning, Tommy and Lizzy wait, not speaking, outside the still-closed video store.

*[EXT. RAIL BRIDGE. DAY

A train speeds across.

INT. TRAIN. DAY

Sick Boy, Tommy, Spud and Renton sit drinking from an extensive carry-out.

SICK BOY
This had better be good.

TOMMY
It will be. It'll make a change for three miserable junkies who don't know what they want to do with themselves since they stopped doing smack.

SICK BOY
If I'm giving up a whole day and the price of a ticket, I'm just saying it had better be good. There's plenty of other things I could be doing.

TOMMY
Such as?

SICK BOY
Such as sitting in a darkened room, watching videos, drinking, smoking dope and wanking. Does that answer your question?

They sit in silence.]

EXT. STATION. DAY

The station is in the middle of a moor. There appears to be no habitation around. In the distance are some hills.

The train stands at the station.

As it pulls away, Renton, Spud, Tommy and Sick Boy are left standing on the platform, looking around.

SICK BOY
Now what?

*Cut from completed film.

TOMMY

We go for a walk.

SPUD

What?

TOMMY

A walk.

SPUD

But where?

Tommy points vaguely across the moor.

TOMMY

There.

SICK BOY

Are you serious?

They step across the tracks towards the vast moorland. They stop.

All but Tommy sit down on rocks or clumps of heather.

TOMMY

Well, what are you waiting for?

SPUD

I don't know, Tommy. I don't know if it's . . . normal.

A group of three serious Walkers trudge past from the other end of the platform, decked out in regulation Berghaus from head to foot. They tramp off towards the wilderness. The boys watch them go.

Spud opens a can.

TOMMY

It's the great outdoors.

SICK BOY

It's really nice, Tommy. Can we go home now?

TOMMY

It's fresh air.

SICK BOY

Look, Tommy, we know you're getting a hard time off Lizzy, but there's no need to take it out on us.

TOMMY

Doesn't it make you proud to be Scottish?

RENTON

I hate being Scottish. We're the lowest of the fucking low, the scum of the earth, the most wretched, servile, miserable, pathetic trash that was ever shat into civilization. Some people hate the English, but I don't. They're just wankers. We, on the other hand, are colonized by wankers. We can't even pick a decent culture to be colonized by. We are ruled by effete arseholes. It's a shite state of affairs and all the fresh air in the world will not make any fucking difference.

The three serious Walkers are receding into the distance.

The boys troop back towards the platform.

(*voice-over*)

At or around this time, we made a healthy, informed, democratic decision to get back on drugs as soon as possible. It took about twelve hours.

46

INT. SWANNEY'S FLAT. DAY

Renton hands over money to Swanney.

Renton then begins cooking up.

Also present and cooking or shooting up are Spud, Swanney, Allison and Baby, and Sick Boy.

> RENTON
> (*voice-over*)

It looks easy, this, but it's not. It looks like a doss, like a soft option, but living like this, it's a full-time business.

   He injects.

INT. SHOP. DAY

Renton, Spud and Sick Boy are stuffing objects into their shirts and pockets.

INT. SWANNEY'S FLAT. DAY

Renton lies back, narcotized.

EXT. STREET. DAY

Renton and Spud are running along the street.

Two uniformed Store Detectives are running after them.

Sick Boy stands in a doorway. As the Detectives run past, he strolls away in the opposite direction.

INT. SWANNEY'S FLAT. DAY

Renton lies back as before.

> SICK BOY

Ursula Andress was the quintessential Bond girl. That's what everyone says. The embodiment of his superiority to us: beautiful, exotic, highly sexual and yet unavailable to everyone but him. Shite. Let's face it: if she'd shag one punter from Edinburgh, she'd shag the fucking lot of us.

47

INT. SWANNEY'S FLAT. LATER

Spud cooks up, watched by Swanney.

Nearby lie the drugged forms of Renton, Sick Boy and Allison and Baby.

INT. RENTON FAMILY HOME, LIVING-ROOM. NIGHT

Renton's Mother and Father sit reading the paper and a magazine.

INT. RENTON FAMILY HOME, PARENTS' BEDROOM. NIGHT

Renton trawls through drawers and any containers (shoe boxes, make-up boxes, under the mattress, etc.) until he finds some cash/jewellery.

INT. SWANNEY'S FLAT. DAY

Renton lies back, staring vacantly ahead.

Tommy flops down beside him. Renton shows barely a flicker of awareness.

> TOMMY
> Lizzy's gone, Mark, she's gone and fucking dumped me. It was the video tape and that Iggy Pop business and all sorts of other stuff. She told me where to go and no mistake. I said, is there any chance of getting back together, like, but no way, no fucking way.

INT. HOSPITAL WARD SITTING-ROOM. DAY

A few elderly patients sit in armchairs watching daytime television.

Renton and Spud jump and climb through an open window. Watched by the helpless patients, they calmly disconnect the television and take it with them as they leave by the same route.

INT. SWANNEY'S FLAT. DAY

Renton and Tommy slumped side by side as before.

> TOMMY
> I want to try it, Mark. You're always going on about how it's the ultimate hit and that. Better than sex. Come on, I'm a fucking adult. I want to find out for myself.

48

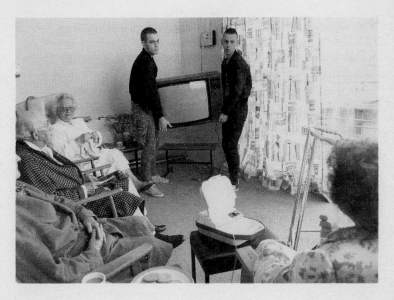

49

Renton huddles up and leans away from Tommy.

I've got the money.

Tommy produces ten pounds from his pocket.

EXT. STREET. DAY

Renton and Spud run along the street.

INT. SWANNEY'S FLAT. DAY

Tommy lies drugged on the floor.

INT. FLAT TO BE BURGLED. DAY

The door of an ordinary flat is kicked open.

Begbie walks in, crowbar in hand, followed by Sick Boy and Spud.

INT. SWANNEY'S FLAT. DAY

SICK BOY

Honor Blackman a.k.a. Pussy Galore, what a total fucking misnomer. I wouldn't touch her with yours. I'd sooner shag Col Kreb. At least you know where you are with a woman like that. Not much to look at, like, but personality, that's what counts, that's what keeps a relationship going through the years. Like heroin. I mean, heroin's got fucking great personality.

Sick Boy opens the heel of his shoe to reveal a syringe.

*[INT. FLAT TO BE BURGLED, LIVING-ROOM. DAY

Begbie and Sick Boy turn the flat over in search of anything to steal.]

INT. SWANNEY'S FLAT. DAY

Swanney hands over a small bag of heroin in exchange for ten pounds from Renton.

*Cut from completed film.

*[INT. FLAT TO BE BURGLED, KITCHEN. DAY

Spud checks the fridge and pulls out a large chunk of deep-frozen meat.

He hits with the crowbar until it fractures and splits. Inside there is some jewellery.]

INT. CAR. DAY

The car is empty. A window is broken and the door opened.

The car alarm goes off.

Renton reaches under the seat and finds the radio/cassette. He then pulls the bonnet release.

EXT. CAR. DAY

The car alarm rings on until Renton calmly produces a pair of wire cutters and a spanner to cut free and release the battery.

The alarm is silenced.

Renton walks away with the battery and the stereo.

INT. GP'S SURGERY. DAY

RENTON
(*voice-over*)

Swanney taught us to adore and respect the National Health Service, for it was the source of much of our gear. We stole drugs, we stole prescriptions, or bought them, sold them, swapped them, forged them, photocopied them or traded them with cancer victims, alcoholics, old age pensioners, AIDS patients, epileptics and bored housewives. We took morphine, diamorphine, cyclozine, codeine, temazepam, nitrezepam, phenobarbitone, sodium amytal dextropropoxyphene, methadone, nalbuphine, pethidine, pentazocine, buprenorphine, dextromoramide chlormethiazole. The streets are awash with drugs that you can have for unhappiness and pain, and we took them all. Fuck it, we would have injected Vitamin C if only they'd made it illegal.

*Cut from completed film.

The GP examines Renton's chest and smiles.

The GP turns to wash his hands. Renton pulls on his shirt and steals a prescription pad off the desk.

*[INT. SWANNEY'S FLAT. DAY

Renton lies back with his eyes closed. A football enters the frame to bounce off his head and out again.

He opens his eyes and it happens again.

Opposite him, Spud, Sick Boy and Tommy stand looking down on him.

Tommy throws the ball again.]

INT. PUB I. DAY

It's the first day of the Edinburgh Festival.

Renton, Tommy, Spud, Sick Boy and Begbie sit drinking.

They observe a young male American Tourist walk in in a bulky red anorak and glasses. He goes past them towards the toilet.

Begbie stands up.

INT. PUB I, TOILET. DAY

The American Tourist turns from the urinal to see Begbie, Renton, Sick Boy, Spud and Tommy approaching. Begbie punches and kicks the Tourist and pulls out a knife.

*[INT. TAXI. DAY

The door of the taxi opens. Begbie, Tommy, Spud, Sick Boy and Renton get in, carrying the red anorak and glasses.

As the taxi pulls away they study the photograph in the passport. They look at one another in agreement.

*Cut from completed film.

EXT. TAXI. DAY

The taxi motors along.]

INT. PUB I. NIGHT

A man at the bar is now wearing the red anorak.

Begbie divides up the money among Sick Boy, Tommy, Spud and Renton.

Renton takes his share.

>   BEGBIE
> And remember, Rents: no skag.

>   RENTON
> Aye, OK, Franco.

>   RENTON
>   (*voice-over*)
> But the good times couldn't last for ever.

INT. SWANNEY'S FLAT. DAY

Renton lies as before. Around the room are Swanney, Allison, Tommy, Spud and Sick Boy.

Allison begins screaming and wailing.

Slowly, the others rouse themselves to varying degrees.

RENTON
(*voice-over*)

I think Allison had been screaming all day, but it hadn't really registered before. She might have been screaming for a week for all I knew. It's been days since I've heard anyone speak, though surely someone must have said something in all that time, surely to fuck someone must have?

SICK BOY

What's wrong, Allison?

Allison points towards the bundle of dirty blankets in which her baby is wrapped. Sick Boy follows her directions.

SPUD

Calm down, calm down. It's going to be all right, everything's going to be just fine.

RENTON
(*voice-over*)

Nothing could have been further from the truth. In point of fact, nothing at all was going to be just fine. On the contrary, everything was going to be bad. Bad? I mean worse than it already was.

Sick Boy stands over the bundle. The baby is dead.

SICK BOY

Oh, fuck.

Sick Boy reaches out to Allison.

RENTON
(*voice-over*)

It wasn't my baby. She wasn't my baby. Baby Dawn. She wasn't mine. Spud's? Swanney's? Sick Boy's? I don't know. Maybe Allison knew. Maybe not. I wished I could think of something to say, something sympathetic, something human.

Say something, Mark, say something –

RENTON

I'm cookin' up.

There is a silence.

Renton begins scrambling around through the works.

ALLISON

Cook one for me, Renton. I need a hit.

RENTON
(*voice-over*)

And so she did, I could understand that. To take the pain away. So I cooked up and she got a hit, but only after me. That went without saying.

EXT. STREET. DAY

Renton, Spud and Sick Boy cross the road to approach the shop.

RENTON
(*voice-over*)

Well, at least we knew who the father was now. It wasn't just the baby that died that day. Something inside Sick Boy was lost and never returned. It seemed he had no theory with which to explain a moment like this.

*[INT. SHOP. DAY

Renton, Spud and Sick Boy are stuffing their pockets, as seen before.

Renton's theft is interrupted by Diane's voice.

DIANE

Hello there, Mark.

Diane is standing just beside him.

What are you doing?

---

*Cut from completed film.

Renton is speechless, but a few stolen items fall from inside his jacket down to the floor.

Diane looks down.

Spud and Sick Boy start to snigger.

One of the Store Detectives become aware of the group. He starts walking towards them.

You didn't tell me you were a thief.

> SPUD

Hey, go easy, lady. The boy's got a habit to support.

> SICK BOY

Opium doesn't just grow on trees, you know.

A few more items fall from Renton's jacket as the Store Detective closes in.

Renton looks at Diane.]

EXT. STREET. DAY

Renton and Spud are running, pursued by the Two Store Detectives.

> RENTON
> (*voice-over*)

Nor did I. Our only response was to keep on going and fuck everything. Pile misery upon misery, heap it up on a spoon and dissolve it with a drop of bile, then squirt it into a stinking purulent vein and do it all over again. Keep on going: getting up, going out, robbing, stealing, fucking people over, propelling ourselves with longing towards the day it would all go wrong.

As seen in the opening scene, Renton is nearly hit by a car that screeches to a halt as he crosses a road.

He looks at the driver, at Spud running away and the Store Detectives approaching.

> (*voice-over*)

Because no matter how much you stash or how much you steal, you never have enough. No matter how often you go out and rob and fuck people over, you always need to get up and do it all again.

Renton smiles and waits.

(*voice-over*)
Sooner or later, this sort of thing was bound to happen.

One of the Detectives runs straight past him, after Spud.

The other Detective crashes into Renton with a mighty punch in the stomach.

INT. COURT. DAY

Spud and Renton stand in the dock. Renton's Mother and Father, Sick Boy, Begbie and Spud's Mother (Mrs Murphy) are among those in the gallery.

The Sheriff delivers his sentence.

SHERIFF
. . . because shoplifting is theft, which is a crime, and, despite what you may believe, there is no such entity as victimless crime. Heroin addiction may explain your actions, but it does not excuse them. Mr Murphy, you are a habitual thief, devoid of regret or remorse. In sentencing you to six months' imprisonment my only worry is that it will not be long before we meet again. Mr Renton, I understand that you have entered into a programme of rehabilitation in an attempt to wean yourself away from heroin. The suspension of your sentence is conditional upon your continued cooperation with this programme. Should you stand guilty before me again, I shall not hesitate to impose a custodial sentence.

RENTON
Thank you, your honour. With God's help, I'll conquer this affliction.

The Sheriff and Renton stare at one another for a moment. Renton turns to look at Spud, then back towards the Sheriff, who is now leaving the court.

(*voice-over*)
What can you say? Well, Begbie had a phrase for it.

INT. PUB I. DAY

The pub is crowded. Around Renton are his Mother, Father, Begbie, Sick Boy and Gav.

BEGBIE

It was fucking obvious that that cunt was going to fuck some cunt.

There is a round of nodding and 'poor Spud'ing. Everyone begins to talk at once.

FATHER

I hope you've learned your lesson, son.

MOTHER

Oh, my son, I thought I was going to lose you there. You're nothing but trouble to me, but I still love you.

BEGBIE

Clean up your act, sunshine. Cut that shite out for ever.

MOTHER

You listen to Francis, Mark, he's talking sense.

BEGBIE

Fucking right and I am. See, inside, you wouldn't last two fucking days.

SICK BOY

There's better things than the needle, Rents. Choose life.

He winks.

MOTHER

I remember when you were a baby, even then you would never do what you were told.

BEGBIE

But he pulled it off, clever bastard, and he got a result.

They laugh, then fall silent.

Renton turns around. Behind him stands Spud's mother.

RENTON

Mrs Murphy, I'm sorry about Spud. It wasn't fair, him going down and not me –

Tears in her eyes, Mrs Murphy turns and walks away.

Renton watches her go. Behind him Begbie shouts.

BEGBIE

It's no our fault. Your boy went down because he was a fucking smack-head and if that's not your fault, I don't know what is.

Begbie turns back to Renton.

Right. I'll get the drinks in.

He moves towards the bar.

Renton slips away.

Renton walks through the bar towards the toilets, then out of a back door.

EXT. YARD. DAY

Renton emerges into a narrow yard surrounded by a high wall. He looks around. The steel back gate is locked.

RENTON
(*voice-over*)
I wished I had gone down instead of Spud. Here I was surrounded by my family and my so-called mates and I've never felt so alone, never in all my puff. Since I was on remand they've had me on this programme, the state-sponsored addiction, three sickly sweet doses of methadone a day instead of smack. But it's never enough, and at the moment it's nowhere near enough. I took all three this morning and now I've got eighteen hours to go till my next shot and a sweat on my back like a layer of frost. I need to visit the mother superior for one hit, one fucking hit to get us over this long, hard day.

Renton climbs the wall. He stands on top, then dives off the other side, executing a somersault in mid-air.

INT. SWANNEY'S FLAT. NIGHT

Swanney is cooking up.

Renton lands on the floor behind him like a gymnast.

RENTON
What's on the menu this evening?

SWANNEY
Your favourite dish.

RENTON
Excellent.

SWANNEY
Your usual table, sir?

RENTON
Why, thank you.

Renton sits on his usual cushion on the floor.

SWANNEY

And would sir care to settle his bill in advance?

RENTON

Stick it on my tab.

SWANNEY

Regret to inform, sir, that your credit limit was reached and breached a long time ago.

RENTON

In that case –

He produces twenty pounds.

SWANNEY

Oh, hard currency, why, sir, that'll do nicely.

He swipes the notes underneath a UV forgery checker.

Can't be too careful when we're dealing with your type, can we?

Renton begins his search for a vein.

Would sir care for a starter? Some garlic bread perhaps?

RENTON

No, thank you. I'll proceed directly to the intravenous injection of hard drugs, please.

SWANNEY

As you wish.

He hands Renton the syringe. Renton injects, then lies back on the dirty, red, carpeted floor.

He lies completely still. His pupils shrink. His breathing becomes slow, shallow and intermittent.

He sinks into the floor until he is lying in a coffin-shaped and coffin-sized pit, lined by the red carpet.

Swanney stands over him.

SWANNEY

Perhaps sir would like me to call for a taxi?

An ambulance siren becomes faintly audible.

INT. SWANNEY'S STAIRWELL. NIGHT

The siren is a little louder.

Swanney holds Renton under his arms and drags him backwards down the steps.

EXT. STREET. NIGHT

As Swanney emerges, still dragging Renton, the siren grows louder and then an ambulance speeds by without stopping.

Swanney drags Renton across the pavement and into the open door of a waiting taxi.

Swanney then steps out of the taxi's other door, pausing only to tuck a ten-pound note into Renton's pocket before closing the door.

INT. TAXI. NIGHT

Renton lies on the floor of the taxi, as Swanney left him, rolling slightly as the taxi takes a corner.

EXT. HOSPITAL/TAXI. NIGHT

The taxi is stationary.

We do not see the driver's face but his hand opens the door and then drags Renton out on to the pavement by his ankles before taking the ten-pound note, getting back in the cab and driving away.

Renton lies on the pavement.

Two Porters lift him by arms and ankles on to a trolley.

We do not see the Porters' faces as they wheel Renton into the hospital.

INT. HOSPITAL ACCIDENT AND EMERGENCY DEPARTMENT. NIGHT

Renton is wheeled through the department, then into a bay surrounded by a white nylon curtain.

INT. TROLLEY BAY. NIGHT

The Porters lift Renton from one trolley on to another, then leave him alone in the bay surrounded by the curtain.

Renton lies alone. His breathing is still shallow and erratic. Around him is the usual accident and emergency paraphernalia: blood pressure machine, oxygen tap, bandages, etc.

A Doctor comes in and gives Renton an injection, then leaves.

DOCTOR

Wake up. Wake up.

Renton breathes more easily.

*[*The Two Porters return with another trolley. They lift Renton roughly on to it and wheel him away.*

INT. HOSPITAL CORRIDOR. NIGHT

The Porters wheel Renton along.

INT. WARD. NIGHT

The Porters lift Renton off the trolley and dump him on the bed.

A nurse sticks a thermometer in his mouth.

INT. WARD. DAY

Renton's Father and Mother lift Renton, now fully conscious, off the bed and dump him in a wheelchair.

INT. HOSPITAL CORRIDOR. DAY

Mother walks ahead. Behind her, Father pushes Renton in the wheelchair.]

INT. TAXI. DAY

Mother and Father sit either side of Renton.

*Cut from completed film.

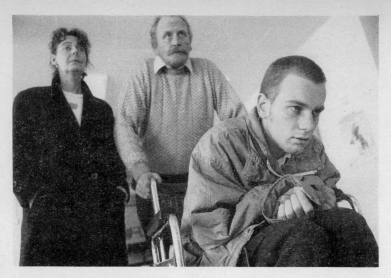

INT. RENTON'S BEDROOM. DAY

Father shoves Renton on to the bed, then walks out past Mother, who looks at Renton for a moment before closing the door.

INT. OTHER SIDE OF RENTON'S BEDROOM DOOR. DAY

Renton's Father's hand slides three bolts across to lock the door.

INT. RENTON'S BEDROOM. DAY

Renton lies on the bed.

> RENTON
> (*voice-over*)

I don't feel the sickness yet, but it's in the post, that's for sure. I'm in the junky limbo at the moment, too ill to sleep, too tired to stay awake, but the sickness is on its way. Sweat, chills, nausea, pain and craving. Need like nothing else I have ever known will soon take hold of me. It's on its way.

The door opens. Renton's Mother walks in with a bowl of soup and a piece of bread. Father watches from the doorway.

MOTHER

We'll help you, son. You'll stay with us until you get better. We'll beat this together.

RENTON

Maybe I could go back to the clinic.

MOTHER

No. No clinics, no methadone. That made you worse, you said so yourself. You lied to us, son, your own mother and father.

RENTON

At least get us some Temazepam.

MOTHER

No, you're worse coming off that than you are with heroin. Nothing at all.

FATHER

It's a clean break this time.

MOTHER

You're staying where we can keep an eye on you.

RENTON

I do appreciate what you're trying to do, I really do, but I need just one score, to ease myself off it. Just one. Just one.

Mother retreats past Father, who closes the door. The bolts go home again.

Renton lies back and closes his eyes. His forehead is damp with sweat.

He begins to shake.

He tosses and turns, becoming wrapped up in a swathe of blankets. As he unravels them, he is astonished to find a fully clothed Begbie in the bed with him.

BEGBIE

Well, this is a good laugh, you fucking useless bastard. Go on, sweat that shite out of your system, because if I come back and it's still there, I'll fucking kick it out.

Begbie laughs and covers himself up.

Renton rips away the blankets, but Begbie has gone.

Renton looks up.

Baby Dawn is crawling across the ceiling.

Renton looks down to see Diane sitting on the end of the bed.

Diane sings 'Temptation' by New Order.

DIANE

'Oh, you've got green eyes, oh, you've got red eyes, and I've never met anyone quite like you before.'

Renton looks back up. Dawn continues her slow crawl, leaving behind a thick trail of unidentifiable slime.

Renton looks down. Sick Boy sits on the end of the bed, holding a cup of tea and a chocolate biscuit.

Mother stands behind him.

SICK BOY

It's a mug's game, Mrs Renton. I'm not saying I was blameless myself, far from it, but there comes a time when you have to turn your back on that nonsense and just say no.

Sick Boy takes a bite of his biscuit.

Dawn crawls on. She has fangs now.

Spud sits on the end of the bed, in a caricature prison uniform with arrows on it, plus a ball and chain.

Dawn has claws as well.

Tommy sits on the end of the bed. He looks terrible.

TOMMY

Better than sex, Rents, better than sex. The ultimate hit. I'm a fucking adult. I'll find out for myself. Well, I'm finding out all right.

Renton looks up again just as the baby drops on to his face. He tears her off and throws her into a corner.

Renton's Mother and Father are washing him. Mother bends down and picks up the large, damp sponge from the corner, where it landed. She wipes her son's face with it.

FATHER

Mark, there's something you need to do.

*[INT. CONSULTING ROOM. DAY

A Doctor stands up as Renton enters.

DOCTOR

Come in. Sit down, please.

They both sit down.

Well, you've already spoken to one of our counsellors, but before we go on there're just a few questions I'd like to ask you.]

INT. RENTON FAMILY HOME, LIVING-ROOM. DAY

Renton, his Mother and Father sit watching television.

INT. STUDIO. DAY

Renton is sitting inside a plastic booth shaped like a giant syringe.

The Doctor, now dressed as a game-show host, stands in front, with Renton's Mother and Father beside him.

DOCTOR

Question number one: the human immunodeficiency virus is a – what?

FATHER

Retrovirus?

DOCTOR

Retrovirus is the correct answer.

Fanfare.

Question number two: HIV binds to which receptor on the host lymphocyte? Which receptor?

*Cut from completed film.

Mother and Father confer.

CD4.

CD4 receptor is the correct answer.

Fanfare.

And now, question number three: is he guilty or not guilty?

He's our son.

Is the correct answer.

Fanfare.

And now it's time to 'Take the Test'.

Lights flash. Music. A garish Hostess walks on with two envelopes. She holds them out for Mother to choose one.

INT. CONSULTING ROOM. DAY

The Doctor watches in silence as the Hostess, now dressed as a medical technician, draws blood from Renton's arm and puts it in a tube. She marks the tube with a pre-printed, numbered label.

INT. STUDIO. DAY

Mother opens one of the envelopes. She is speechless with joy.

The plastic booth opens up. Lights flash again, etc.

Renton steps out.

INT. SOCIAL CLUB. NIGHT

Renton, his Mother and Father sit at a table in the local social club. It is a Saturday night and the club is busy.

Everyone sits in rapt silence. It is not initially clear what is going on. Near the bar a Caller with a microphone calls over the PA –

Two and four, twenty-four . . . seven . . . fifteen . . . clickety-
click, sixty-six –

And so on, as he draws the numbers from the drum.

*Everyone studies their cards, except Renton, who studies the people
instead, his drink untouched.*

*The number-calling continues until suddenly interrupted by Mother's
voice.*

MOTHER

Mark . . . Mark, you've got a house. House! House! For
goodness' sake, Mark.

They bustle around him and pass his card to the front.

RENTON
(*voice-over*)

It seems, however, that I really am the luckiest guy in the world.
Several years of addiction right in the middle of an epidemic,
surrounded by the living dead, but not me – I'm negative. It's
official. And once the pain goes away, that's when the real battle
starts. Depression. Boredom. You feel so fucking low, you'll want
to fucking top yourself.

His mother counts a wad of money in front of him.

EXT. HOUSING ESTATE. DAY

*On the door of a flat 'plaguer', 'HIV' and 'junky AIDS scum' are
daubed on the walls.*

*The sound of a ball being regularly bounced against a wall can be
heard.*

INT. TOMMY'S FLAT. NIGHT

It is poorly furnished. Tommy is seated.

*Renton has the football, which he kicks against the wall and catches,
then drops and kicks again, and so on. The ball is slightly flat.*

RENTON

Are you getting out much?

TOMMY

No.

RENTON

Following the game at all?

TOMMY

No.

RENTON

No. Me neither.

Renton drops the ball. It rolls to a halt in the corner.

He sits down.

TOMMY

You take the test?

RENTON

Aye.

TOMMY

Clear?

RENTON

Aye.

TOMMY

That's nice.

RENTON

I'm sorry, Tommy.

TOMMY

Have you got any gear on you?

RENTON

No, I'm clean.

TOMMY

Well, sub us, then, mate. I'm expecting a rent cheque.

Renton produces some of his bingo win.

As he hands the notes over, their eyes and hands meet for a moment.

Tommy puts the money away.

Thanks, Mark.

RENTON

No problem.

(*voice-over*)

No problem – easy to say when it's some other poor cunt with shite for blood.

*[INT. HOSPITAL. NIGHT

Renton walks along a corridor and into a ward.

INT. WARD. DAY

Sheets cover the lower half of Swanney in bed.

They are thrown back to reveal the stump of an above-knee amputation.

*Cut from completed film.

71

SWANNEY

Surprise! Pa-pah!

Renton sits down and takes it in silence.

Hit the artery by mistake. Common enough error, or so the quack
tells us, as though that's going to make my leg grow back. Still, it
could have been worse, it could have been my fucking dick. And I
tell you what, in this place you get looked after: clean sheets,
regular meals and all the morphine you can eat.

RENTON

Great.

SWANNEY

And see when I get out of here. I've got plans. Going to get myself
straightened out and head off to Thailand, where women really
know how to treat a guy. See, out there you can live like a king if
you've got white skin and a few crisp tenners in your pocket. No
fucking problem.

RENTON

Sure.

SWANNEY

The strategy is this: get clean, get mobile, get into dealing, and
this time next year I'll be watching the rising sun with a posse of
oriental buttocks parked on my coupon.

RENTON

Sounds great, Swanney.

SWANNEY

Yeah.

RENTON

You'll have to send us a postcard.

SWANNEY

Sure will, pal, sure will.

EXT. PARK. DAY

Renton and Sick Boy are seated in their firing patch, sitting on plastic bags with beer, vodka, hash and the cassette player. The airgun is present as before but they are not making any use of it.

SICK BOY

Eughh. Sounds horrible.

RENTON

It wasn't that bad.

SICK BOY

Did he – you know?

RENTON

What?

SICK BOY

You know.

RENTON

No, he didn't make me touch it.

SICK BOY

Oh no, don't even mention it.

RENTON

He made me lick it.

SICK BOY

God, you're sick.

RENTON

And I got a stitch stuck between my teeth, jerked my head back and the whole fucking stump fell off.

SICK BOY

Cut it out.

RENTON

When are you going to visit him?

SICK BOY

Don't know. Maybe Thursday.

RENTON

You're a real mate. And what about Tommy? Have you been to see him yet?

Sick Boy is silent. He stiffens as he avoids Renton's gaze. They shift fractionally apart.

Renton tuts.

SICK BOY

Fuck you. OK, so Tommy's got the virus. Bad news, big deal. The gig goes on, or hadn't you noticed? Swanney fucks his leg up. Well, tough shit, but it could have been worse.

RENTON

You're all heart.

SICK BOY

I know a couple of addicts. Stupid wee lassies. I feed them what they need. A little bit of skag to keep them happy while the punters line up at a fiver a skull. It's easy money for me. Not exactly a fortune, but I'm thinking, 'I should be coining it here.' Less whores, more skag. Swanney's right. Get clean, get into dealing, that's where the future lies. Set up some contacts, get a good load of skag, punt it, profit. What do you think?

RENTON

Fuck you.

SICK BOY

And I'll tell you why. Because I'm fed up to my back teeth with losers, no-hopers, draftpacks, schemies, junkies and the like. I'm getting on with life. What are you doing?]

INT. RENTON'S BEDSIT. NIGHT

Renton sits alone on the bed, making a joint and reading a book.

There is a knock at the door.

Renton answers the door.

Diane is standing in the common passageway in her school uniform.

They stand in silence for a moment.

                    RENTON
What do you want?

                    DIANE
Are you clean?

                    RENTON
Yes.

                    DIANE
Is that a promise, then?

                    RENTON
Yes, as a matter of fact, it is.

                    DIANE
Calm down, I'm just asking. Is that hash I can smell?

                    RENTON
No.

                    DIANE
I wouldn't mind a bit, if it is.

                    RENTON
Well, it isn't.

                    DIANE
Smells like it.

                    RENTON
You're too young.

                    DIANE
Too young for what?

   Renton looks in each direction along the empty passageway.

INT. RENTON'S BEDSIT. NIGHT

Renton and Diane are lying in the bed.

Diane, wearing one of Renton's T-shirts, is rolling a mega-joint quite unaware of the scrutiny of Renton.

DIANE

You're not getting any younger, Mark. The world is changing, music is changing, even drugs are changing. You can't stay in here all day dreaming about heroin and Ziggy Pop.

RENTON

It's Iggy Pop.

DIANE

Whatever. I mean, the guy's dead anyway.

RENTON

Iggy Pop is not dead. He toured last year. Tommy went to see him.

DIANE

The point is, you've got to find something new.

Diane completes the joint.

RENTON
(*voice-over*)

She was right. I had to find something new. There was only one thing for it.

EXT. LONDON. DAY

A contemporary retake of all those 'Swinging London' montages: Red Routemaster/Trafalgar Square/Big Ben/Royalty/City gents in suits/ Chelsea ladies/fashion victims/Piccadilly Circus at night.

Intercut with close-ups of classic street names on a street map (all the ones made famous by Monopoly).

INT. ESTATE AGENT'S OFFICE. DAY

The montage ends on one street, then draws back to reveal the whole map of London pinned to a wall.

A Man holding a telephone walks in front of the map and belches loudly.

Revealing more, he is in a scruffy, cramped office with half a dozen occupied desks and twice as many telephones. Seated at the one nearest to the belching Man is Renton. He is wearing a shirt and tie now. He turns in response to the belch.

MAN

Can you take this call?

Renton takes the telephone and reaches for a piece of paper from which he reads.

RENTON

Hello, yes, certainly. It's a beautifully converted Victorian town house. Ideally located in a quiet road near to local shops and transport.

Renton checks his watch.

EXT. THE AI IN NORTH LONDON. DAY

Renton stands waiting beside this busy London road, outside some very unfortunate housing, as the traffic streams past.

RENTON
(*voice-over*)

Two bedrooms and a kitchen/diner. Fully fitted in excellent decorative order. Lots of storage space. All mod cons. Three hundred and twenty pounds per week.

A couple approach.

Renton unlocks the door of a flat and holds the door open while he ushers them in.

INT. LONDON FLAT. DAY

Renton shows the Couple round a typical London flat nightmare. A poor conversion, poor decor, everything small and ill-fitting. The windows rattle as the traffic roars by.

RENTON
(*voice-over*)

I settled in not too badly and I kept myself to myself. Sometimes, of course, I thought about the guys, but mainly I didn't miss them at all. After all, this was boom town where any fool could make cash from chaos and plenty did. I quite enjoyed the sound of it all.

Profit, loss, margins, takeovers, lending, letting, subletting, subdividing, cheating, scamming, fragmenting, breaking away. There was no such thing as society and even if there was, I most certainly had nothing to do with it. For the first time in my adult life I was almost content.

INT. LONDON BEDSIT. NIGHT

Renton finishes eating a pot noodle. He puts it down and picks up a letter. He lies back and reads.

Intercut with:

INT. SCHOOLROOM. DAY

A class is in progress. A teacher lectures to a mixed class, but Diane is not listening as she is writing.

EXT. SCHOOL DAY

Diane is leaving the school when Sick Boy catches up with her. They stop and then she walks away.

EXT. PARK. DAY

Diane walks along a concrete path. As she does so she has to step over Spud, who lies asleep/unconscious beside the remains of a carry-out.

DIANE
(*voice-over*)

Dear Mark, I'm glad you've found a job and somewhere to live. School is fine at the moment. I'm not pregnant but thanks for asking. Your friend Sick Boy asked me last week if I would like to work for him but I told him where to go. I met Spud, who sends his regards, or at least I think that's what he said. No one has seen Tommy for ages. And finally, Francis Begbie has been on television a lot this week –

INT. LONDON BEDSIT. NIGHT

Renton turns the page

DIANE
(*voice-over*)

as he is wanted by the police in connection with an armed robbery in a jeweller's in Corstorphine. Take care. Yours with love, Diane.

There is a buzz at the door. Renton re-examines the letter. There is another buzz.

RENTON

Oh no.

INT. HALLWAY OUTSIDE BEDSIT. NIGHT

Renton opens the door to an unseen figure. It is Begbie.

INT. BEDSIT. NIGHT

Renton sits on the bed. Begbie stands over him, pointing a gun at his head.

He pulls the trigger. It clicks harmlessly.

BEGBIE

Armed robbery? With a replica? How can it be armed robbery? It's a fucking scandal.

He 'fires' the gun a few times at his own head, then chucks it to the floor.

And the haul. Look.

He digs a few rings out of his pocket and throws them to Renton.

Solid silver, my arse. I took it to a fence – it's trash, pure trash. There's young couples investing all their hopes in that stuff, and what are they getting?

RENTON

It's a scandal, Franco.

BEGBIE

Too right it is. Now look, have you got anything to eat, 'cos I'm fucking Lee Marvin, by the way.

79

INT. BEDSIT. DAY

Begbie is sitting on the bed in his underwear, eating cereal while watching television. A small carry-out is nearby.

Renton finishes dressing for work. He pauses at the open door, looking back towards his guest.

> RENTON
> (*voice-over*)

Begbie settled in in no time at all.

> *Begbie opens a can of beer. Renton closes the door.*

INT. HALLWAY OUTSIDE BEDSIT. DAY

Renton closes his door. He is about to walk away when he hears Begbie shouting.

> BEGBIE
> (*from the bedsit*)

Rents, Rents, come fucking back here.

> *Renton opens the door. Begbie is holding out an empty packet of cigarettes.*

Look.

> RENTON

What?

> BEGBIE

I've no fucking cigarettes.

> *Begbie throws the packet down to the floor. It lands near the door. He has turned back to the television and takes a swig of beer.*

> RENTON

Right.

> *Renton closes the door again.*

INT. BEDSIT. NIGHT

Renton and Begbie lie in the single bed with their heads at opposite ends.

Begbie snores. Renton is wide awake, with a pair of smelly-socked feet only inches from his nose.

> RENTON
> (*voice-over*)

Yeah, the guy's a psycho, but it's true, he's a mate as well, so what can you do?

INT. LONDON BEDSIT. DAY

Where the first empty packet of cigarettes fell to the floor there is now a large heap of empty packets: the product of weeks at sixty a day.

Another one lands on the pile.

Begbie, still in his underwear, still can in hand, sits watching the racing as before.

Behind him, cigarettes and alcohol are stacked up like a miniature duty-free warehouse.

Renton sits behind him, reading a book.

> BEGBIE

Hey, I'm wanting a bet put on.

> RENTON

Can you not go yourself?

> BEGBIE

I'm a fugitive from the law. I can't be seen on the fucking streets. Now watch my lips. Kempton Park. Two-thirty. Five pounds to win. Bad Boy.

INT. HALLWAY OUTSIDE BEDSIT. DAY

The door opens, Renton walks out, the door closes and Renton walks away.

A wild, frightening scream erupts from beyond the door.

INT. LONDON BEDSIT. DAY

Begbie, alone in the bedsit, is screaming a cry of primal joy.

RENTON
(*voice-over*)

Bad Boy came in at 16 to 1. And with the winnings, we went out to celebrate.

INT. LONDON PARTY. NIGHT

To loud music and strobing, fractured lights, surrounded by dry ice, Begbie dances near a tall woman.

Other people dance nearby.

Begbie gives the thumbs-up to Renton, who sits on a stool at one side drinking from a bottle of beer. Begbie and the Woman walk away.

Renton looks around the club at the various men and women.

RENTON
(*voice-over*)

Diane was right. The world is changing, music is changing, drugs are changing, even men and women are changing. One thousand years from now there'll be no guys and no girls, just wankers. Sounds great to me. It's just a pity that no one told Begbie.

EXT. STREET. NIGHT

A car sits in a street near the club, windows steamed up.

INT. CAR. NIGHT

Begbie and the Woman embrace passionately.

The Woman undoes Begbie's trousers.

INT. PARTY. NIGHT

Renton's gaze continues to wander around.

RENTON
(*voice-over*)

You see, if you ask me, we're heterosexual by default, not by decision. It's just a question of who you fancy.

INT. CAR. NIGHT

Begbie and the Woman continue their embrace as she unbuttons his shirt.

> RENTON
> (*voice-over*)

It's all about aesthetics and it's fuck all to do with morality.

> *Suddenly Begbie freezes. He is holding the 'Woman's' groin. There is something there that shouldn't be.*

> *Begbie goes crazy, simultaneously trying to put his clothes back on, hit the Woman and get out of the car.*

EXT. STREET. NIGHT

Begbie stumbles away from the car, pulling up his trousers as he goes.

> RENTON
> (*voice-over*)

But you try telling Begbie that.

INT. BEDSIT. NIGHT

Begbie sits on the bed.

Renton is sitting on the floor watching.

> BEGBIE

I'm no a fucking buftie and that's the end of it.

> RENTON

Let's face it, it could have been wonderful.

> *Begbie leaps off the bed, grabs Renton and head-butts him, then holds him by the lapel.*

> BEGBIE

Now, listen to me, you little piece of junky shit. A joke's a fucking joke, but you mention that again and I'll cut you up. Understand?

> *Begbie produces his knife.*

> *There is a knock at the door.*

They do not move.

There is another knock.

INT. BEDSIT. NIGHT

Begbie lies sleeping on the bed. There are two sets of feet by his head, one on each side.

At the other end lie Renton (awake) and Sick Boy (asleep).

> RENTON
> (*voice-over*)

Since I last saw him, Sick Boy had reinvented himself as a pimp and a pusher and was here to mix business and pleasure, setting up 'contacts', as he constantly informed me, for the great skag deal that was one day going to make him rich.

*[INT. ESTATE AGENT'S OFFICE. DAY

Renton sits at his desk, haggard and tired.

Other people bustle around him. Telephones ring, etc.

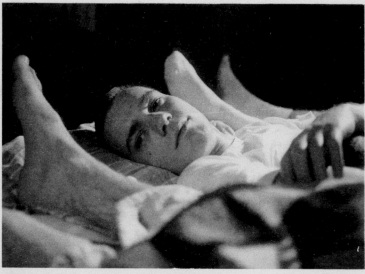

*Cut from completed film.

In the background the Man (who belched) is trying to promote a flat down the telephone.

> MAN

Beautifully converted Victorian town house. Ideally located in a quiet road near to local shops and transport. Two bedrooms and a kitchen/diner. Fully fitted in excellent decorative order. Lots of storage space. All mod cons. Three hundred and twenty pounds per week.]

INT. BEDSIT. NIGHT

Renton (still dressed for work), Begbie and Sick Boy sit in a line on the bed with fish suppers laid out on their laps, but Renton's is untouched.

> SICK BOY

Good chips.

> RENTON

I can't believe you did that.

> SICK BOY

I got a good price for it. Rents, I need the money.

> RENTON

It was my fucking television.

> SICK BOY

Well, Christ, if I'd known you were going to get so humpty about it, I wouldn't have bothered. Are you going to eat that?

He takes Renton's fish supper and adds it to his own.

Have you got a passport?

> RENTON

Why?

> SICK BOY

Well, this guy I've met runs a hotel. Brothel. Loads of contacts. Does a nice little sideline in punting British passports to foreigners. Get you a good price.

RENTON

Why would I want to sell my passport?

SICK BOY

It was just an idea.

INT. LEFT LUGGAGE ROOM. DAY

Renton drops his passport into an envelope and throws the envelope into a locker.

He turns the key and pockets it.

RENTON
(*voice-over*)

I had to get rid of them. Sick Boy didn't do his drug deal and he didn't get rich. Instead, he and Begbie just hung around my bedsit looking for things to steal. I decided to put them in the worst place in the world.

EXT. BUSY LONDON ROAD. DAY

Traffic floods past as before.

INT. LONDON FLAT. DAY

Inside the flat that Renton showed the couple around.

Sick Boy and Begbie are standing in the hallway.

Renton is in the open doorway. He throws them the keys and leaves.

INT. LONDON BEDSIT. NIGHT

The cramped bedsit is a mess, filled with litter and unwashed clothes.

Renton lies on his bed, content to be alone.

INT. LONDON FLAT. NIGHT

The flat is in darkness. The door opens and a figure enters. It is the Man from Renton's office.

RENTON
(*voice-over*)
But, of course, they weren't paying any rent, so when my boss
found two desperate suckers who would, Sick Boy and Begbie
were bound to feel threatened.

Man is followed by another couple.

He switches on a light.

MAN
As you can see, it's a beautiful conversion. Two bedrooms,
kitchen/diner. Fully fitted. Lots of storage. All mod cons. Three
hundred and twenty quid a week.

From nowhere, Begbie and Sick Boy spring out at him.

*[INT. BEDSIT. DAY

*Renton looks around the stripped, empty bedsit one last time before
closing the door as he leaves.*]

RENTON
(*voice-over*)
And that was that. But by then we had another reason to go back.
Tommy.

EXT. RAILWAY. DAY

An InterCity train speeds by.

INT. TOMMY'S FLAT. NIGHT

A kitten sits on the floor.

GAV
(*voice-over*)
Tommy knew he had the virus, like, but never knew he'd gone
full-blown.

*Cut from completed film.

RENTON
(*voice-over*)

What was it, pneumonia or cancer?

GAV
(*voice-over*)

No, toxoplasmosis. Sort of like a stroke.

RENTON
(*voice-over*)

Eh? How's that?

INT. CREMATORIUM CHAPEL. DAY

A service is in progress. Those present include Renton and Gav, who are engaged in hushed conversation, Begbie, Spud, Sick Boy and Lizzy.

GAV

He wanted to see Lizzy again.

He indicates Lizzy.

Lizzy wouldn't let him near the house. So he bought a present for her, brought her a kitten.

RENTON

I bet Lizzy told him where to put it.

GAV

Exactly. I'm not wanting a cat, she says. Get to fuck, right. So there's Tommy stuck with this kitten. You can imagine what happened. The thing was neglected, pissing and shitting all over the place. Tommy was lying around fucked out of his eyeballs on smack or downers. He didn't know you could get toxoplasmosis from cat shit.

RENTON

I didn't either. What the fuck is it?

GAV

Fucking horrible. Like an abscess on your brain.

RENTON

Fucking hell. So what happened?

88

INT. TOMMY'S FLAT. DAY

The kitten as before.

Slow track back to reveal more.

GAV
(*voice-over*)
He starts getting headaches, so he just uses more smack, for the
pain, like. Then he has a stroke. A fucking stroke. Just like that.
Got home from hospital and died about three weeks later. Been
dead for ages before the neighbours complained about the smell
and the police broke the door down. Tommy was lying face down
in a pool of vomit.

The lower half of Tommy's clothed body is visible.

INT. CREMATORIUM CHAPEL. DAY

The coffin travels away. Gav and Renton watch it go.

GAV
The kitten was fine.

INT. PUB I. NIGHT

*Gav, Renton, Spud, Sick Boy, Begbie and a few others are gathered in
the pub, still dressed in their funeral garb. They are drinking and
talking.*

*[SPUD
Every time I think of Tommy I think of Australia, because every
time I went round he was just lying there, junked out of his mind,
watching Aussie soaps. Until he sold the telly, of course, then he
was just lying there. But every time I think of him I still think of
Australia.]

*There is a short silence before Spud begins softly singing 'Two Little
Boys'. He finishes unaccompanied.*

*Cut from completed film.

INT. SWANNEY'S FLAT. NIGHT

Spud, Begbie and Renton are seated.

Sick Boy is handing round bottles of beer before he too sits down.

They are all still wearing their funeral garb.

Renton raises his bottle.

RENTON

Tommy.

> *They all drink.*

SICK BOY

Did you tell him?

BEGBIE

No. On you go.

RENTON

What?

SICK BOY

There's a mate of Swanney's. Mikey Forrester – you know the guy. He's come into some gear. A lot of gear.

RENTON

How much?

SICK BOY

About four kilos. So he tells me. Got drunk in a pub down by the docks last week, where he met two Russian sailors. They're fucking carrying the stuff. For sale there and then, like. So he wakes up the next morning, realizes what he's done and gets very fucking nervous. Wants rid of this. *[He's looking for Swanney to punt it, but Swanney's nowhere to be seen since he lost his leg.]

RENTON

So?

SICK BOY

So he met me and I offered to take it off his hands at a very

*Cut from completed film.

reasonable price, with the intention of punting it on myself to a
guy I know in London.

RENTON

So we've just come from Tommy's funeral and you're telling me
about a skag deal?

BEGBIE

Yeah.

There is silence.

RENTON

What was your price?

SICK BOY

Four grand.

RENTON

But you don't have the money?

SICK BOY

We're two thousand short.

RENTON

That's tough.

SICK BOY

Come on, Mark, every cunt knows you've been saving up down in
London.

RENTON

Sorry, boys, I don't have two thousand pounds.

BEGBIE

Yes, you fucking do. I've seen your statement.

RENTON

Jesus.

BEGBIE

Two thousand, one hundred and thirty-three pounds.

RENTON

Four kilos. That's what – ten years' worth? Russian sailors? Mikey
Forrester? What the fuck are you on these days? You've been to

jail, Spud, so what's the deal – like it so much you want to go back again?

SPUD

I want the money, Mark, that's all.

BEGBIE

If everyone keeps their mouth shut, there'll be no one going to jail.

*[EXT. STREET. DAY

Renton is visible first, apparently talking to himself, then Diane.

RENTON

It's so simple. We buy it at four grand, we punt it at twenty to this guy that Sick Boy knows, and he punts it on at sixty. Everyone's happy, everyone's in profit. I put up two. I come away with six.

DIANE

Unless you get caught.

RENTON

So long as everyone keeps their mouths shut, we'll not be getting caught.

DIANE

So why have you told me about it?

RENTON

Well, you're not going to tell anyone, are you, and besides, I thought we could meet up afterwards, maybe go somewhere together.

DIANE

I've got a boyfriend, Mark.

RENTON

What? steady like?

DIANE

That's right: 'going steady' for four weeks now.

*Cut from completed film.

RENTON

And what age are you? Thirteen? Fourteen?

DIANE

Sixteen next month.

RENTON

Happy birthday.

DIANE

What do you think – I should be carrying a torch for you?

Renton thinks it over.

RENTON

So what's he like?

DIANE

Well, he's young and he's healthy.

They both laugh.

And you're such a deadbeat, Mark.]

INT. SWANNEY'S FLAT. DAY.

Heroin is in the process of being prepared for injection: heated, drawn up, etc.

An arm is prepared for injection: sleeve rolled up, tourniquet bound, veins tapped, etc.

Mikey Forrester, Sick Boy, Spud and Begbie look on.

RENTON
(*voice-over*)

I hadn't told anyone everything that was running through my mind about what might happen in London. There were a lot of possibilities I didn't want to talk to anyone about. Ideas best kept to myself. What no one told me was that when we bought the skag, some lucky punter would have to try it out. Begbie didn't trust Spud and Sick Boy was too careful these days, so I rolled up my sleeve and did what had to be done.

Renton injects the heroin into a vein in his arm.

RENTON

It's good, it's fucking good.

*[EXT. BUS STATION. NIGHT

Renton walks past a Beggar huddling against a wall.

The Beggar's sign reads: 'FALKLANDS VETERAN. I LOST MY LEG FOR MY COUNTRY. PLEASE HELP.'

The beggar is Swanney.]

RENTON
(*voice-over*)

Yes, that hit was good. I promised myself another one before I got to London – just for old time's sake, just to piss Begbie off.

EXT. ROAD. NIGHT

The bus travels towards London.

INT. BUS NIGHT

Sick Boy dabs at amphetamine.

Spud drinks.

INT. BUS TOILET. NIGHT

Renton cooks up in the bus toilet.

RENTON
(*voice-over*)

This was to be my final hit. But let's be clear about this: there's final hits and final hits. What kind was this to be? *[Some final hits are actually terminal one way or another, while others are merely transit points as you travel from station to station on the junky journey through a junky life.]

*Cut from completed film.

94

INT. BUS. NIGHT

Begbie sits grimly. The others are relaxed.

RENTON
(*voice-over*)

This was his nightmare. The dodgiest scam in a lifetime of dodgie scams being perpetrated with three of the most useless and unreliable fuck-ups in town. I knew what was going on in his mind: any trouble in London and he would dump us immediately, one way or another. He had to. If he got caught with a bag full of skag, on top of that armed robbery shit, he was going down for fifteen to twenty. Begbie was hard, but not so hard that he didn't shite it off twenty years in Saughton.

BEGBIE

Did you bring the cards?

SICK BOY

What?

BEGBIE

The cards. The last thing I said to you was mind the cards.

SICK BOY

Well, I've not brought them.

BEGBIE

It's fucking boring after a while without the cards.

SICK BOY

I'm sorry.

BEGBIE

Bit fucking late, like.

SICK BOY

Well, why didn't you bring them?

BEGBIE

Because I fucking told you to do that, you doss cunt.

SICK BOY

Christ.

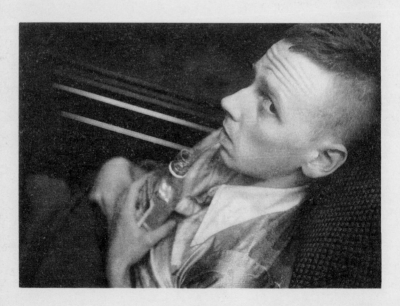

96

EXT. LONDON. DAY

The bus travels through London.

EXT. STREET. DAY

The gang enter a cheap hotel. Begbie's bag contains the heroin.

INT. HOTEL. DAY

They are met by Andreas, a man in his late thirties of Mediterranean appearance.

He shakes Sick Boy's hand.

ANDREAS

These are your friends?

SICK BOY

These are the guys I told you about.

ANDREAS

OK.

SICK BOY

Is he here?

97

ANDREAS

Yes, he's here. I hope you didn't get followed or nothing.

BEGBIE

We didn't get followed.

Andreas leads them along a corridor and into a room.

INT. HOTEL ROOM. DAY

An unexceptional Man is waiting.

Andreas leaves the room and closes the door.

Begbie opens the bag and produces the two slabs of heroin.

The Man opens both and tastes the heroin.

He produces a set of kitchen scales from his bag and weighs the two bags.

RENTON
(*voice-over*)

Straight away he clocked us for what we were: small-time wasters with an accidental big deal.

MAN

So what do you want for it?

BEGBIE

Twenty thousand.

MAN

But it's not worth more than fifteen.

BEGBIE

Nineteen.

The man shakes his head and lights a cigarette.

MAN

Nineteen I can't offer you, I'm sorry.

RENTON
(*voice-over*)

This was a real drag to him. He didn't need to negotiate. I mean,

98

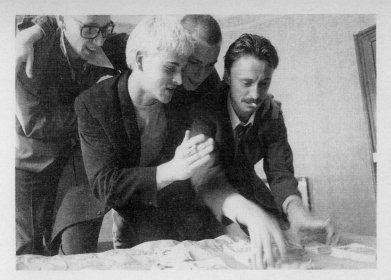

what the fuck were we going to do if he didn't buy it? Sell it on the streets? Fuck that.

The deal is done. The Man hands over the money and waits as it is counted, then leaves with the drugs.

(voice-over)

We settled on sixteen thousand pounds. He had a lot more in the suitcase, but it was better than nothing. And just for a moment it felt really great, like we were all in it together, like friends, like it meant something. A moment like that, it can touch you deep inside, but it doesn't last long, not like sixteen thousand pounds.

INT. LONDON PUB. DAY

The pub is crowded with afternoon drinkers.

Renton, Spud, Sick Boy and Begbie sit drinking. Begbie is still keeping a firm hand on the sports bag, which now holds the money.

SICK BOY

So what are you planning with your share, Spud?

RENTON

Buy yourself that island in the sun?

99

For four fucking grand? One palm tree, a couple of rocks and a sewage outflow.

I don't know, maybe I'll buy something for my ma, and then buy some good speed, no bicarb like, then get a girl, take her out like, and treat her – properly.

Shag her senseless.

No, I don't mean like that – I mean something nice, like, that's all –

You daft cunt. If you're going to waste it like that, you might as well leave it all to me. Now get the drinks in.

I got a round already.

I got the last one.

It's your round, Franco.

Begbie stands up.

OK. Same again?

I'm off for a pish. When I come back, that money's still here, OK?

The moment you turn your back, we're out that door.

Sick Boy walks away towards the toilet.

I'll be right after you.

BEGBIE

You'll never catch us, you flabby bastard. Right, see, when I come
back –

RENTON

We'll be half-way down the road with the money.

BEGBIE

I'd fucking kill you.

RENTON

I guess you would, Franco.

Begbie walks away to the bar.

Spud and Renton look at each other and the bag of money.

Are you game for it?

*Spud looks at the bag and around the pub towards the toilet door and
Begbie.*

Begbie stands at the bar, awaiting the pints.

Well?

SPUD

Are you serious?

Renton looks around.

RENTON

I don't know. What do you think?

Spud says nothing. Suddenly they are interrupted.

SICK BOY

Still here, I see.

Sick Boy sits down.

RENTON

Yes, well, we wouldn't run out on a mate.

SICK BOY

Why not? I know I would. Where's Franco?

Renton turns to see Begbie making his way through the crowd with the pints held precariously.

As he reaches the table a Man standing with a group of friends accidentally nudges Begbie, causing a pint to spill over him.

BEGBIE

For fuck's sake.

MAN

Sorry, mate, I'll get you another.

BEGBIE

All down my fucking front, you fucking idiot.

MAN

Look, I'm sorry, I didn't mean it.

BEGBIE

Sorry's no going to dry me off, you cunt.

RENTON

Cool down, Franco. The guy's sorry.

BEGBIE

Not sorry enough for being a fat cunt.

MAN

Fuck you. If you can't hold a pint, you shouldn't be in the pub, mate. Now fuck off.

Begbie drops the remaining three pints.

As the Man looks down to the falling glasses, Begbie punches him in the face and knees him in the groin.

A fight breaks out between the Man and Begbie.

Sick Boy rushes forward to restrain Begbie.

Renton sits still, not even looking at the fight or what follows. His eyes are fixed on the bag while his hands fiddle.

Begbie stabs Spud in the hand.

                              SPUD
Jesus Christ.

                           SICK BOY
Good one, Franco.

                            BEGBIE
Shut your mouth or you'll be next.

                              SPUD
You've stabbed me, man.

                            BEGBIE
You were in my way.

   Begbie, blade still in hand, addresses the entire pub.

And anyone in my way gets it, fucking gets it. Everybody hear
that? Everybody happy?

   Nobody says anything.

   Renton is seated as before, avoiding Begbie's gaze.

   Begbie addresses him.

Hey, Rent-boy, bring us down a smoke.

   Renton does not move.

                           SICK BOY
We'd better go, Franco.

                              SPUD
I've got to get to the hospital, man.

                            BEGBIE
                           (*to Spud*)
You're not going to any fucking hospital.

                         (*to Sick Boy*)
You're staying there.

                          (*to Renton*)
And you bring me a fucking cigarette.

   Renton swivels and stands up.

                              103

And the bag.

Renton lifts the bag and slowly approaches Begbie.

Renton, nervous, hand shaking, pulls a packet of cigarettes from a pocket and holds it towards Begbie.

Begbie does not move.

Renton holds out the bag.

Begbie takes it.

Now Renton selects a cigarette, puts it in his own lips and finds a lighter in another pocket.

He lights the cigarette and hands it over to Begbie.

Begbie inhales deeply and then blows the smoke towards Renton.

INT. HOTEL ROOM. DAY

Renton lies awake, sharing a bed with Sick Boy, who is asleep.

Spud and Begbie lie on the other, both asleep.

Begbie has an arm draped over the bag, holding it close.

Renton gets up and goes through to the small bathroom.

He puts the light on above the mirror and looks at himself. He washes his face and drinks a glass of water, then walks back to the bedroom.

Renton pulls on his jacket and shoes.

He stands over Begbie, then reaches carefully down to lift Begbie's arm up.

As he does so he realizes that Spud is watching him.

They say nothing.

Renton takes the bag.

Begbie stirs but does not wake.

[Renton looks down at Spud for a moment before unzipping the bag. He pulls out a small wad of cash, which he hands to Spud.

*Cut from completed film.

104

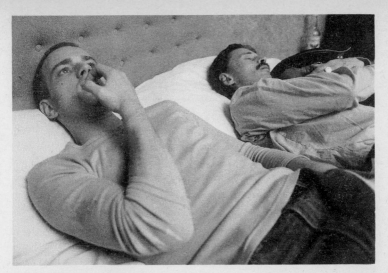

Spud tucks the wad away.]

Renton walks to the door and opens it.

He nods to Spud, then disappears.

INT. LOCKER. DAY

Envelope being removed.

INT. LEFT LUGGAGE. DAY

Renton takes the passport from the envelope.

EXT. STREET. DAY

Renton walks away.

> RENTON
> (*voice-over*)

Now, I've justified this to myself in all sorts of ways: it wasn't a big deal, just a minor betrayal, or we'd outgrown each other, you know, that sort of thing, but let's face it, I ripped them off. My so-called mates. But Begbie, I couldn't give a shit about him, and Sick Boy, well, he'd have done the same to me if only he'd thought of it first, and Spud, well, OK, I felt sorry for Spud – he never hurt anybody.

INT. HOTEL. DAY

Prostitutes, punters, Sick Boy and Spud line the corridor as two Policemen walk past towards:

INT. HOTEL ROOM. DAY

Begbie goes radge.

EXT. STREET. DAY

Renton continues his departure.

RENTON
(*voice-over*)

So why did I do it? I could offer a million answers, all false. The truth is that I'm a bad person, but that's going to change, I'm going to change. This is the last of this sort of thing. I'm cleaning up and I'm moving on, going straight and choosing life. I'm looking forward to it already. I'm going to be just like you: the job, the family, the fucking big television, the washing machine, the car, the compact disc and electrical tin opener, good health, low cholesterol, dental insurance, mortgage, starter home, leisurewear, luggage, three-piece suite, DIY, game shows, junk food, children, walks in the park, nine to five, good at golf, washing the car, choice of sweaters, family Christmas, indexed pension, tax exemption, clearing the gutters, getting by, looking ahead, to the day you die.

CREDITS

CAST

RENTON	Ewan McGregor
SPUD	Ewen Bremner
SICK BOY	Jonny Lee Miller
TOMMY	Kevin McKidd
BEGBIE	Robert Carlyle
DIANE	Kelly Macdonald
SWANNEY	Peter Mullan
MR RENTON	James Cosmo
MRS RENTON	Eileen Nicholas
ALLISON	Susan Vilder
LIZZY	Pauline Lynch
GAIL	Shirley Henderson
GAVIN (AND US TOURIST)	Stuart McQuarrie
MIKEY	Irvine Welsh
GAME SHOW HOST	Dale Winton
DEALER	Keith Allen
ANDREAS	Kevin Allen
GAIL'S MOTHER	Annie Louise Ross
GAIL'S FATHER	Billy Riddoch
DIANE'S MOTHER	Fiona Bell
DIANE'S FATHER	Vincent Friel
MAN 1	Hugh Ross
MAN 2	Victor Eadie
WOMAN	Kate Donnelly
SHERIFF	Finlay Welsh
ESTATE AGENT	Eddie Nestor

CREW

Director	Danny Boyle
Producer	Andrew Macdonald
Screenplay	John Hodge
Director of Photography	Brian Tufano
Editor	Masahiro Hirakubo
Production Designer	Kave Quinn
Costume Designer	Rachel Fleming

Production Manager	Lesley Stewart
Casting	Gail Stevens
	Andy Pryor
Make-up Design	Graham Johnston
Art Director	Tracey Gallacher
First Assistant Director	David Gilchrist
Special Visual Effects	Grant Mason
	Tony Steers
Sound Recordist	Colin Nicolson
Second Assistant Director	Claire Hughes
Third Assistant Director	Ben Johnson
Script Supervisor	Anne Coulter
Floor Runners	Aidan Quinn
	Michael Queen
Production Accountant	Jennifer Booth
Production Coordinator	Shellie Smith
Assistant to the Producer	Jill Robertson
Production Runner	Kirstin McDougall
Location Manager	Robert How
Location Assistant	Saul Metzstein
Construction Manager	Colin H. Fraser
Set Dresser	Penny Crawford
Scenic Artist	Stuart Clarke
Draughtspersons	Jean Kerr
	Frances Connell
Assistant Art Director	Niki Longmuir
Art Department Assistants	Irene Harris
	Lorna J. Stewart
Art Department Runners	Miguel Rosenberg-Sapochnik
	Alan Payne
Art Department Trainee	Stephen Wong
Focus Puller	Robert Shipsey
Clapper Loader	Lewis Buchan
Grip	Adrian McCarthy
Steadicam Operator	Simon Bray
Camera Trainee	Neil Davidson
Boom Operator	Tony Cook
Sound Maintenance Engineer	Noel Thompson
Assembly Editor	Anuree de Silva
Assistant Editors	Neil Williams
	Denton Brown
FT2 Editing Trainee	Rab Wilson

Re-Recording Mixers	Brian Saunders
	Ray Merrin
	Mark Taylor
Effects Editor	Jonathan Miller
Dialogue Editor	Richard Fettes
Footsteps Editor	Martin Cantwell
Prop Master	Gordon Fitzgerald
Dressing Props	Piero Jamieson
	Mat Bergel
Standby Props	Stewart Cunningham
	Scott Keery
Construction Chargehand	Derek Fraser
Standby Carpenter	Bert Ross
Standby Stagehand	Brian Boyne
Carpenters	Brian Adams
	Richard Hassall
	Peter Knotts
	John Watt
Painters	James Patrick
	Paul Curren
	Bobby Gee
Stagehand	John Donnelly
Plasterer	Paterson Lindsay
Props Driver	Gregor Telfer
Props Trainees	Paul McNamara
	Michelle Bowker
Underwater Cameraman	Mike Valentine
Underwater Camera Assistant	Jim Kerr
Make-up and Hair	Robert McCann
Wardrobe Supervisor	Stephen Noble
Gaffer	Willie Cadden
Best Boy	Mark Ritchie
Electricians	Mark Ritchie
	Jimmy Dorigan
Genny Operator	John Duncan
Stills Photography	Liam Longman
Stunt Arranger	Terry Forrestal
Stunt Performers	Tom Delmar
	Nrinder Dhudwar
	Richard Hammatt
	Paul Heasman
	Tom Lucy

	Andreas Petrides
Special Technical Adviser	Eamon Doherty
Location Manager – London	Andrew Bainbridge
Location Assistant – London	Charlies Hiscott
London Contact	Lene Bausager
Action Vehicles	Robbie Ryan
Tracking Vehicles	Bikers of Coddenham Ltd
Facility Vehicles and Drivers	Bristol Television Film Services Ltd
Animal Handler	David Stewart
Camera Car Driver	Eric Smith
Caterers	Guy Cowan
	Fiona Cowan
	Allan Bell
	Jackie Douglas
	Isabel Graham
	Andy Irvine
	John McVeigh
Security	Dennis McFadden
	William Adams
	James Dunsmuir
	William Mackinnon
	Ian Miller
Completion Bond	Film Finances Ltd
Production Solicitors	Jonathan Berger
	Mishcon de Reya
Insurance	Sampson & Allen
Titles Design	Tomato
Opticals	Cine Image
Colour by	Rank Film Laboratories
Post Production Sound	The Sound Design Co.
Editing Facilities	Salon
Caterers	Reel Food
Arriflex camera and Zeiss lenses supplied by	Media Film Service London
Additional Camera Equipment	ICE
Lighting Equipment	Lee Lighting (Scotland) Ltd
Video Transfers	Midnight Transfer
Publicity	McDonald & Rutter
Originated on	Eastman Colour Film from Kodak
Freight	Ecosse World Express
Fido Services by	Cinesite Digital Film Center

Sound re-recorded at Delta Sound Services

Thanks to David Aukin, Allon Reich, Sara Geater, Carol Anne Docherty,
Archie Macpherson, Jonathan Channon, Nicole Jacob, Kay Sheridan,
Richard Findlay at Tods Murray WS.
Special thanks to David Bryce, Eamon Doherty and all at Calton
Athletic Recovery Group for their inspiration and courage.

SOUNDTRACK AVAILABLE ON EMI RECORDS

'Lust for Life'
Words and music by Iggy Pop/David Bowie
Performed by Iggy Pop
Published by EMI Music Publishing Ltd/EMI Virgin Music Ltd/
Tintoretto Music administered by RZO Music
Courtesy of Virgin Records American Inc.

'Carmen – Habañera'
Composed by Georges Bizet
Courtesy of Laserlight/KPM

'Deep Blue Day'
Written by Brian Eno/Daniel Lanois/Roger Eno
Performed by Brian Eno
Published by Opal Music/Upala Music Inc./BMI
Courtesy of Virgin Records Ltd

'Trainspotting'
Words and music by Bobby Gillespie/Andrew Innes/Robert Young/
Martin Duffy
Performed by Primal Scream
Published by EMI Music Publishing Ltd/Complete Music Ltd
Courtesy of Creation Records Ltd

'Temptation'
Words and music by Ian Marsh/Martyn Ware/Glen Gregory
Performed by Heaven 17
Published by EMI Virgin Music Ltd/Sound Diagrams Ltd/Warner
Chappell Music Ltd
Courtesy of Virgin Records Ltd

113

'Mile End'
Written by Banks/Cocker/Doyle/Mackey/Senior/Webber
Performed by Pulp
Published by Island Music Ltd
Courtesy of Island Records Ltd

'For What You Dream of (Full on Renaissance Mix)'
Written by John Digweed/Nick Muir/Carol Leeming
Performed by Bedrock featuring Kyo
Published by Seven PM Music/Sony Music Publishing/
Peermusic (UK) Ltd
Courtesy of Stress Recordings

'2.1'
Written by Donna Lorraine Matthews
Performed by Elastica
Published by EMI Music Publishing Ltd
Courtesy of DGC Records and Deceptive Records Ltd

'Hertzlich tut mich verlangen'
Composed by J S Bach
Performed by Gabor Lehotka
Courtesy of Laserlight/KPM

'Two Little Boys'
Words and music by Edward Madden/Theodore Morse
Performed by Ewen Bremner
Published by Herman Darewski Music Publishing Co/EMI Publishing Ltd/
Redwood Music Ltd (Carlin)

'A Final Hit'
Written by Neil Barnes/Paul Daley
Performed by Leftfield
Published by Hard (UK) Hands Publishing Ltd/Chrysalis Music Ltd
Courtesy of Hard Hands/Columbia Records
by arrangement with Sony Music Entertainment (UK) Ltd

'Statuesque'
Song and words by Wener
Music by Wener, Stewart, Maclure, Osman
Performed by Sleeper
Published by Sony Music Publishing
Courtesy of Indolent Records/BMG Records (UK) Ltd

'Born Slippy (Nuxx)'
Words and music by Rick Smith/Karl Hyde
Performed by Underworld
Published by Sherlock Holmes Music Ltd
Courtesy of Junior Boy's Own, London

'Closet Romantic'
Written by Damon Albarn
Performed by Albarn, Gauld, Sidwell, Henry, Smith
and The Duke Strings Quartet
Published by MCA Music Ltd
Licensed by EMI Records Ltd by courtesy of Parlophone and EMI
Special Markets UK

Television Clips
Archie Gemmill goal
Courtesy of Worldmark
Horseracing
Courtesy of International Racecourse Management Ltd

Filmed on location in Glasgow, Edinburgh and London

The story, all names, characters and incidents portrayed in this
production are fictitious. No identification with actual persons, places,
buildings and products is intended or should be inferred.

A Figment Film in association with Noel Gay Motion Picture
Company Ltd
for Channel Four

© Channel Four Television Corporation
MCMXCV

Danny Boyle with Irvine Welsh

AFTERWORD –
INTERVIEW WITH IRVINE WELSH

This interview with Irvine Welsh was conducted during the film's penultimate week of shooting. Welsh had flown over especially from Amsterdam, where he now lives, to do a cameo performance as the drug dealer Mikey Forrester.

KEVIN MACDONALD: *Did you ever consider when you were writing the book, or when it was published, that it might be turned into a film?*
IRVINE WELSH: I never even considered that the book would be published in the first place – I never thought about it in terms of publication – so getting it published was a big enough surprise, it being successful was a surprise and then it being made into a play was a surprise and now it being made into a film is a surprise. So it's just been a series of different surprises that I've become quite inured to. I don't see what can possibly happen to it next. Surely this has to be the end!

KM: *When Andrew, Danny and John got in touch with you and said they were interested in doing the film, what was your immediate response?*

IW: I thought it was quite brave of them to do because, especially with the success of *Shallow Grave*, they could have taken big bucks in Hollywood. I couldn't really see it as a film at first just because of it being episodic and not a strong kind of narrative thing. But on the other hand, I couldn't see it as a play before it became a successful play, so it's got an appeal. I think that a lot of people are sick of the kind of representations of the world that we live in as a kind of bland *Four Weddings and a Funeral* sort of place – they want something that says a wee bit more about the society that we actually live in and a wee bit more about the different cultures within that society that tend to be ignored.

KM: *Do you think that the film will be faithful to your book?*
IW: I think that as an author the first thing you have to tell yourself is: I wrote the book but somebody else is making the film. The whole point of it – the exciting part of it – is that it's going to be transformed in some way. The more transformation the better from my point of view. People go on about a 'faithful interpretation', but you can't have a faithful interpretation of something; you can maybe have it in spirit, but it's going to change as it moves into a different medium. I think that with film or any other different medium, you don't have the same degree of freedom as you maybe do with the blank page, on to which you can put whatever you like. You can build up a lot of psychological depth to the characters in a book, whereas in film you've really got to take a line on it and say, maybe, is this a black comedy or is this social realism? And then stick to that line. Anyway, that's the exciting part about it: how people are going to see it, how they're going to interpret it. It is open to so many different interpretations, and it's something that I change my own mind about quite a lot.

KM: *Are you glad that they haven't taken the social realist approach?*
IW: Yes, I am kind of happy with that. I think I would have been a wee bit despondent if – not to knock Ken Loach or anything because I think that he's brilliant at what he does – if they had made it in the Loach fashion because I don't think we need another Ken Loach. I would have been disappointed if it had been a kind of worthy piece of social realism. I think there's more to it than that. It's about the culture and the lifestyle in a non-

judgemental way. It's about how people live their lives and how people interact. To see it as just a kind of reaction to social oppression, to social circumstances, is to rip some of the soul out of it and to make the characters into victims. I don't think that they really are. I think that they're people whose ideals and ambitions perhaps outstrip what society has to offer them, but I think they've got great strength in spite of that.

KM: *How did you find performing in the film?*
IW: You admire the discipline that actors have. I've now worked a fair bit with actors over the year and I used to think of it as very much a bunch of people poncing around on stage. But the effort, the concentration and work that goes into it from the actors and the whole crew . . . you see really what a sweaty, grafting kind of work-intensive industry it is. It destroys my stereotype that I had about actors, theatre, film people, all of that, of being a bit kind of effeminate. The reality is very different.

KM: *Were you surprised when Danny asked you to do this little cameo?*
IW: I wasn't surprised in a sense. It's something that I would have done if I'd been him because its effective. It stops the author from criticizing the film because you can't say, 'Oh, my God, they've ruined my book!' because you've been a part of the whole process and you've joined in. That's a kind of frivolous thing to say, but I think that it always adds a bit of intrigue.

KM: *What part are you playing?*
IW: I'm playing this drugs dealer who's probably one of the least sympathetic characters in the book. He's a kind of pretty manipulative, nasty, horrible guy, so a lot of people will say typecasting again!

KM: *Do you think that* Trainspotting – *the book – is dated in any way?*
IW: Yes, it's dated in the context of Edinburgh because the whole drug scene has changed slightly there. It's still a 'Class A' drug society, but there's fewer people who are doing smack these days and who are into that hard-core subculture . . . it's being managed through methadone programmes. That use of heroin had moved through to Glasgow. Probably up until a couple of years ago *Trainspotting* was more applicable to Glasgow than it was to

Edinburgh. The thing had moved. But the drug which people chose to fuck up on isn't really the issue. The fact is that there's just so few opportunities for people that it's not surprising that they try to escape from it or try to obliterate as much of the pain of the world as possible. So while the drugs may have changed, the issues are just the same. People have always abused drugs. Traditionally it's been alcohol, now it's a cocktail of different drugs simply because there are different drugs available. It doesn't really matter whether it's heroin or alcohol or whatever. In fact, you're probably better off being a junkie than an alcoholic because if you're a junkie you can reform quite successfully if you just change the people that you're hanging around with. It's very difficult for an alcoholic to do that because you're being bombarded with these messages all the time about drinking and it's so much a part of the culture, whereas you can move out of the smack subculture.

KM: *So it's not a period piece?*
IW: No. If you're being pedantic about it, you could say that it was set in Edinburgh between 1982 and 1988, but the issues of drug addiction and drug abuse and the on-going HIV issues are as pertinent as ever – probably more so now.

KM: *What was your opinion of* Shallow Grave *– and did you think the makers of that film had the right abilities or vision for a film of* Trainspotting?
IW: Yes. I only saw *Shallow Grave* a couple of days ago on video – it's just been a series of coincidences that I didn't see it when I was in Britain, and then I moved to Holland and then when it came to Holland it was only there for a day before I was off to the States. But I have seen a video of it. What appealed to me about *Shallow Grave* was the constant action and movement. I think that sits really well with the bias towards action that modern writing has, that constant motion and movement, keeping things moving and keeping things happening – the kind of visceral, hard-edged humour sits well. The characterizations and characters were completely different and I didn't find the characters particularly empathetic – I couldn't particularly care for the characters – but maybe that's just where I'm coming from. That might just be a class or cultural thing. Everybody I know seemed to feel really sort

of gleeful when Ewan [McGregor] got punched and then got his legs broken! But the other thing I liked about it was the sheer beauty of the camerawork and the use of colours – primary colours. That detail in film-making and that kind of craft and stylization have really been absent in British films, and that was one of the things that really appealed to me.

Shallow Grave

INT. DAY

A blurred image forms on a white screen. A horizontal strip of face, eyes motionless and unblinking.

DAVID
(*voice-over*)
Take trust, for instance, or friendship: these are the important things in life, these are the things that matter, that help you on your way. If you can't trust your friends, well, what then?

EXT. DAWN

A series of fast-cut static scenes of empty streets.

DAVID
(*voice-over*)
This could have been any city: they're all the same.

A rapid, swerving track along deserted streets and down narrow lanes and passageways. Accompanied by soundtrack and credits.

The track ends outside a solid, fashionable Edinburgh tenement.

INT. STAIRWELL. DAY

At the door of a flat on the third floor of the tenement. The door is dark, heavy wood and on it is a plastic card embossed with names of the three tenants. They are Alex Law, David Stevens and Juliet Miller.

A man climbs the stair and reaches the door. He is Cameron Clark, thin and in his late twenties with a blue anorak and lank, greasy hair. He is carrying an awkwardly bulky plastic bag. Cameron gives the doorbell an ineffectual ring and then stands back, shifting nervously from foot to foot until the door is answered.

CAMERON
Hello, I've come about the room.

Cameron enters and the door closes.

INT. LIVING ROOM. DAY

*David, Alex and Juliet sit in a line on the sofa directly opposite
Cameron, who shifts uneasily in his armchair. Alex checks some items
on a clipboard before speaking.*

ALEX

What's his name?

DAVID

I don't know – Campbell or something?

JULIET

Cameron.

ALEX

Cameron?

JULIET

Yes.

ALEX
(to Juliet)

Really?

CAMERON

That's right.

ALEX

(*to Cameron*)

What?

Cameron is not sure what to say.

Well, Cameron, are you comfortable?

CAMERON

Oh, yes, thanks.

ALEX

Good. Well, you've seen the flat?

CAMERON

Yes.

ALEX

And you like it?

CAMERON

Oh, yes, it's great.

ALEX

Yes. It is, isn't it? We all like it. And the room's nice too, don't you think?

CAMERON

Yes.

ALEX

Spacious, quiet, bright, well appointed, all that sort of stuff, all that crap.

CAMERON

Well, yes.

ALEX

So tell me, Cameron, what on earth – just tell me, because I want to know – what on earth could make you think that we would want to share this flat with someone like you?

INT. STAIRWELL. DAY

As Cameron plods slowly down the stairs, his shoes striking out against the stone steps, Alex's criticisms continue.

ALEX
(*voice-over*)

I mean, my first impression, and they're rarely wrong, is that you have none of the qualities that we normally seek in a prospective flatmate. I'm talking here about things like presence, charisma, style and charm, and I don't think we're being unreasonable. Take David here, for instance: a chartered accountant he may be, but at least he tries hard. The point is, I don't think you're even trying.

Cameron has reached the bottom of the stairs. He opens the main door.

And, Cameron – I mean this – good luck!

Cameron leaves and the main door closes behind him.

Do you think he was upset?

*[INT. STAIRWELL. DAY

Outside the door of the flat a prim, matronly Woman in her early twenties rings the bell.

INT. HALL. DAY

Inside the hall of the flat, David approaches the door to open it. Freeze-frame.

ALEX
(*voice-over*)

David likes to keep spare shoelaces in sorted pairs in a box marked, not just 'shoelaces', but 'spare shoelaces'.

David opens the door to the Woman.

WOMAN

I've come to see about the room.

*Cut from completed film.

128

INT. STAIRWELL. DAY

Outside the door of the flat a young Goth girl, aged about twenty, rings the doorbell.

INT. HALL. DAY

Inside the hall of the flat Alex approaches the door to open it. Freeze-frame.

> JULIET
> (*voice-over*)

Alex is a vegetarian. Do you know why? Because he feels it provides an interesting counterpoint to his otherwise callous personality. It doesn't. He thinks he's the man for me. He isn't, though there was a time when, well, there was a time when . . .

Alex opens the door to the Goth.

> GOTH

I've come about this room.

INT. STAIRWELL. DAY

At the door of the flat a Man aged about thirty-five rings the bell.

INT. HALL. DAY

Inside the hall of the flat Juliet approaches the door to open it. Freeze-frame.

> DAVID
> (*voice-over*)

Like one of those stupid posters – you know, a gorilla cuddling a hedgehog, caption 'love hurts' – that's what I think of when I think of Juliet.

Juliet opens the door to the Man.

> MAN

I've come about the room.]

INT. LIVING ROOM. DAY

*In the living room each of the 'candidates' is interviewed individually
with the same seating arrangements as before (i.e. the trio on the sofa
and the applicant on the chair). What we see are briskly intercut
excerpts from each of these interviews. We do not get the responses to the
questions, although we may see some facial reaction.*

All of David's questions are to the Woman.

All of Alex's questions are to the Goth.

All of Juliet's questions are to the Man.

DAVID

All right, just a few questions.

ALEX

I'd like to ask you about your hobbies.

JULIET

Why do you want a room here?

DAVID

Do you smoke?

ALEX

When you slaughter a goat and wrench its heart out with your bare
hands, do you then summon hellfire?

JULIET

I mean, what are you actually doing here? What is the hidden
agenda?

DAVID

Do a little freebase maybe, from time to time?

ALEX

Or maybe just phone out for a pizza?

JULIET

Look, it's a fairly straightforward question. You're either divorced
or you're not.

DAVID

OK, I'm going to play you just a few seconds of this tape – I'd like

you to name the song, the lead singer and three hit singles
subsequently recorded by him with another band.

ALEX

When you get up in the morning, how do you decide which shade
of black to wear?

JULIET

Now, let me get this straight. This affair that you're not having, is
it not with a man or not with a woman?

DAVID

Turning very briefly to the subject of corporate finance – no, this
is important. Leveraged buy-outs – a good thing or a bad thing?

*[
ALEX

With which of the following figures do you most closely identify:
Joan of Arc, Eva Braun or Marilyn Monroe?

JULIET

It's just that you strike me as a man trapped in a crisis of
emotional direction, afflicted by a realization that the partner of
your dreams is, quite simply, just that.]

DAVID

Did you ever kill a man?

ALEX

And when did anyone last say to you these exact words: 'You are
the sunshine of my life'?

*[
JULIET

OK, so A has left you, B is ambivalent, you're still seeing C but D
is the one you yearn for. What are we to make of this? If I were
you, I'd ditch the lot. There's a lot more letters in the alphabet of
love.]

DAVID

And what if I told you that I was the Antichrist?

*Cut from completed film.

131

INT. SQUASH COURT. EVENING

In a sports centre Juliet sits outside a glass-walled squash court. She is ready to play, but at present is watching Alex and David, who are inside the court.

INT. SQUASH COURT. EVENING

Inside the squash court, Alex is about to serve.

ALEX

Squash is often used as a metaphor to represent a struggle for personal domination.

DAVID

Serve.

ALEX

I was trying to educate you.

DAVID

Just serve.

*[ALEX

In the same fashion as chess.

DAVID

What?

ALEX

Chess. Chess is often used as well.

DAVID

Will you shut up and play.

ALEX

You're a bad loser.

DAVID

I haven't lost yet.]

   Alex serves.

*Cut from completed film.

132

INT. SQUASH COURT. EVENING

The squash-court door opens and David walks out past Juliet as Alex stands behind, jabbing his finger at him.

ALEX

Defeat, defeat, defeat – sporting, personal, financial, professional, sexual, everything. Next.

Juliet walks in and closes the door.

INT. SQUASH COURT. EVENING

Inside the squash court Alex is about to serve.

ALEX

Did you know –

JULIET

Just serve, Alex.

Alex serves.

INT. JULIET'S CAR (A MINI). NIGHT

Alex sits in the back, drinking.

Juliet is driving. David sits beside her.

ALEX

I wasn't trying to win.

There is no response from Juliet.

I don't wish to devalue your victory, but I just want you to know: I wasn't trying to win.

DAVID

Victory is the same as defeat. It's giving in to destructive competitive urges.

ALEX

You learn that in your psychotherapy group?

DAVID

Discussion group, Alex, discussion.

JULIET

I thought you stopped going.

ALEX

Yeah, he had too many of those urges. You of all people should know that.

Alex leans close to Juliet. Juliet brakes abruptly and, as Alex flies forwards, elbows him in the chest.

God, you two are just so sensitive. All I'm doing is implying some sort of sordid, ugly, sexual liaison. Why, I'd be proud of that sort of thing.

JULIET

Maybe you should go, Alex. You'll meet someone wonderful.

ALEX

For my life? At a discussion group? I think not.

JULIET

For the flat.

ALEX

No. Be someone else like him. One is enough. And what happened to that girl, that friend of yours, the one that came round. I liked her. I really felt we had something. She could have moved in. We had chemistry.

JULIET

She hated you –

ALEX

Well, she had problems –

JULIET

– more than anyone she has ever met. In her whole life.

ALEX

– I'd be the first to point that out. In all kindness I would. But, like they say, you know, she's got to want to change, hasn't she?

INT. STAIRWELL. DAY

Outside the door of the flat Hugo rings the bell and waits. Juliet opens

*the door. Hugo is in his early thirties, tall, dark and bohemian in
appearance.*

JULIET

You must be Hugo.

HUGO

You must be Juliet.

JULIET

Would you like to come in?

HUGO

I'd be delighted.

*Hugo walks in and Juliet closes the door quite deliberately behind
him.*

INT. VACANT ROOM. DAY

*Hugo looks around, pleased at what he sees, while Juliet watches him.
He sits on the edge of the bed.*

HUGO

It's nice.

JULIET

Would you like to see the rest?

INT. LIVING ROOM. DAY

Hugo is seated on the sofa, Juliet sits opposite on an armchair.

JULIET

What do you do?

HUGO

Well, I've been away for a bit, travelling, that sort of thing, and
now I'm trying to write a novel.

JULIET

What's it about?

HUGO

A priest who dies.

JULIET

I see.

HUGO

Yeah. Well, maybe I'll change it.

JULIET

No.

HUGO

Yes, I mean, who wants to read about another dead priest? It's about some other guy, some guy who's not a priest, who doesn't die. You see, it's better already.

JULIET

Writing seems easy.

HUGO

It's a breeze.

The telephone begins to ring out in the hall. Juliet does not move and at first says nothing. Hugo looks at her and towards the door leading to the hall. After several rings, Juliet speaks.

JULIET

Do you think you could answer that?

136

HUGO

The telephone?

It continues to ring.

JULIET

Yes, the telephone, but if it's for me, I'm not in.

HUGO

You're not in.

JULIET

No.

HUGO

All right.

Hugo stands up. The ringing continues.

INT. HALL. DAY

Hugo lifts the phone. He turns to face Juliet and looks her in the eye as he lies on her behalf.

HUGO

Hello. Yes. Who's calling please? Well, I'm sorry, but she's not in right now. I don't know. Would you like to leave a message?

Hugo replaces the receiver.

It was some guy called Brian.

JULIET

Did he sound upset?

HUGO

A little bit. Is that good or bad?

JULIET

It's an improvement.

The telephone begins to ring again.

HUGO

Shall I answer it?

JULIET

No, just leave it. He knows I must be at home. I'm working nights this week.

The telephone continues to ring.

HUGO

Working nights?

JULIET

I'm a doctor.

HUGO

And he's a patient of yours?

JULIET

No, but he needs treatment.

HUGO

For what?

JULIET

For a certain weakness.

HUGO

The human condition.

JULIET

You know about it?

HUGO

I write about it.

JULIET

And that's not the same thing?

HUGO

No, but like all novelists, I'm in search of the self.

INT. KITCHEN. MORNING

Juliet, dressed and fatigued, sits at the table sipping a cup of coffee. Alex is also seated at the table, but wearing an old dressing-gown and munching at cornflakes while he reads a newspaper and talks at the same time. An array of other papers is spread over the table.

138

ALEX

Has he tried down behind the fridge. I mean, that's where I normally find things.

JULIET

He seemed like a nice guy, Alex.

Juliet gets up and leaves the kitchen. The sound of a bath running is heard.

ALEX

I'm not saying he didn't seem like a nice guy. All I'm saying is, it's a bit strange, and this search for the self, and what's he on about, you know.

Alex hears the mail falling through the door and stands up to leave the kitchen and get it.

JULIET
(*calling from outside*)

He didn't seem strange, Alex. He seemed, you know –

INT. BATHROOM. MORNING

Juliet watches the bath fill.

JULIET

. . . interesting.

INT. KITCHEN, MORNING

Alex considers her reply.

ALEX

Interesting. Interesting.

INT. HALL. MORNING

Alex is walking through the hall to the door, muttering 'interesting' to himself. As he passes the phone it starts to ring. He stops and lifts it.

ALEX

Hello. No, she's not in. No. No. No. No idea.

Alex replaces the receiver and walks on to the door.

139

JULIET
(*from the bathroom*)
Who was it?

ALEX
I don't know. He sounded Swedish. Do you know any Swedish men? Maybe it was just the emotion.

Alex picks up the mail and looks through it. As he does so, David emerges from his room, dressed for work.

What do you think?

DAVID
About what?

ALEX
About this guy, this Hugo person.

DAVID
I don't have time.

ALEX
I'm only asking what you think.

DAVID
I don't have the time to discuss it now. I don't care so long as he's not a freak.

David opens the door. Alex hands him an envelope.

ALEX
This is for you. It's your mother's handwriting, so I didn't open it. I don't like reading about your father's constipation.

David snatches the letter and leaves, closing the door.

Alex walks back across the hall, opening one of the letters and reading it quickly.

JULIET
(*calling from the bathroom*)
So we'll meet him, then?

ALEX
What? Oh, yeah, sure, if you want. I tell you, every letter this guy

140

writes to you is the same: they all begin like pure love and descend into open pornography. 'I dream of your thighs, the soft touch of your white skin leading me in desire, while I, aroused and inflamed –'

Juliet's head and arm appear around the bathroom door. She attempts to grab the letter. Alex plays at holding it just beyond her reach, before letting her take it.

ALEX

Aroused and inflamed.

JULIET

Alex.

ALEX

He even signs them, in his own name, can you believe it? I'd sign someone else's name. I'd sign his name. If I wrote them, that is. Which I don't.

INT. LIVING ROOM. EVENING

Alex, David, Juliet and Hugo sit round a table towards the end of a meal. Alcohol has been consumed. Bowls containing the last of the food sit on the table, being picked at occasionally. Alex dispenses wine mainly into his own glass, alternating with Macallan malt whisky, of which he pours generous measures.

ALEX

Interesting.

HUGO

I see.

ALEX

Yeah, well, that was what she said. Interesting. That's why you're here, you see.

DAVID

Normally I don't meet people, unless I already know them.

HUGO

I see.

DAVID

People can be so cruel.

ALEX

So, uh . . .

HUGO

What?

ALEX

What?

HUGO

You were going to say something.

ALEX

What was I trying to say? Oh, yes, I think, we think, or at least I
suppose we think – am I right?

JULIET

Just get on with it, Alex.

*[DAVID
Keep it going, Alex. You're unstoppable now.]

*Cut from completed film.

142

ALEX

We think it's fine.

Alex starts eating again. The others watch him expectantly. David coughs.

It's OK. There's no problem.

HUGO

You mean I can have the room?

*[ALEX

Well, that's what I said, isn't it?

DAVID

He made it clear.

ALEX

Why, thank you, David.]

JULIET

Yes, you can have the room.

Alex pours yet more alcohol.

ALEX

I'm not usually drunk.

JULIET

Not usually this drunk.

DAVID

Only on expenses.

ALEX

It's true. A newspaper is paying for all this. All this. A newspaper . . .

With exaggerated scorn, Alex knocks over a glass of wine.

JULIET

In a moment he's going to tell you he could have been someone –

ALEX

It was you, Juliet, it was you –

*Cut from completed film.

143

                    JULIET

– instead of what he is –

                    ALEX

What I am.

                    JULIET

– which is –

                    ALEX

– which is a hack.

                    JULIET

The man we know and love.

                    ALEX

A miserable, burnt-out, empty shell of a –

   Alex pauses, looks at his drink, then at Juliet.

Know and love?

                    JULIET

Yeah.

                    ALEX

I think you're lying.

                    JULIET

You're right.

                    ALEX

You see, they don't really know me.

                    JULIET

No, Alex, we don't really love you.

   Alex smiles at Juliet and drinks again.

                    ALEX

Can you afford this place?

                    HUGO

Yeah.

   Hugo reaches into his pocket and pulls out a thick bundle of notes, which he places in front of Alex. Alex leans over and sniffs the notes.

DAVID

Can I ask you a question?

HUGO

Certainly.

DAVID

Have you ever killed a man?

HUGO

No.

DAVID

Well, that's fair enough, then.

Alex raises his head.

ALEX

Certainly smells like the real thing.

EXT. A STREET. NIGHT

At a cash dispenser a man in his thirties is taking out some money.

A younger man, Andy, stands beside him, looking around in a mildly agitated fashion.

As the money emerges, Andy assaults and robs the man. He starts by smashing his victim's face repeatedly against the cash dispenser until the Perspex is smeared with blood. When he has finished and the man lies on the ground, Andy takes the money and the card from the slots, then gets into a car which has pulled up alongside, driven by Tim.

INT. STAIRWELL. DAY

Hugo climbs the stairs, carrying two suitcases. He stops at the door of the flat and looks at a bunch of keys before selecting one, which he inserts in the door.

INT. HALL. DAY

Inside the flat. The door opens and Hugo lifts his cases in, kicking the door closed behind him.

INT. JULIET'S ROOM. DAY

Juliet sleeps, undisturbed by the closing of the door.

INT. HALL. DAY

Hugo walks across the hall and disappears into his room.

*[INT. HUGO'S ROOM. DAY

Hugo unpacks his bags. Included in his things are a few syringes and needles. All these he puts into the drawer beside his bed. He checks inside a second bag.

INT. HALL. DAY

Hugo dials a number on the telephone and awaits a reply.]

INT. JULIET'S ROOM. EVENING

Juliet is woken by her alarm clock. The time is five p.m.

INT. LIVING ROOM. NIGHT

Alex sits watching television, constantly changing channels. Juliet walks in, wearing a dressing gown. She watches Alex for a few moments.

JULIET

Have you seen Hugo?

ALEX

No. Any idea which channel he's on?

INT. HALL. MORNING

The telephone is ringing. Alex lifts the receiver. Again he is wearing his dressing gown and is on his way to pick up the mail.

ALEX

No, she's not in.

Without waiting for any more, he replaces the receiver and walks to the door, where he picks up the mail. On his way back from the door,

*Cut from completed film.

146

David emerges, ready to go to work.

Have you seen him?

                    DAVID
Alex, I don't have the time –

                    ALEX
Yes or no, yes or no, yes or –

                    DAVID
No.

David leaves, slamming the door.

INT. KITCHEN. MORNING

*Alex returns to the kitchen, pausing only to knock at Hugo's door,
which elicits no response. In the kitchen Juliet sits dressed for work,
having just returned. He casually opens an envelope and glances at both
sides of the letter before handing it to her.*

                    ALEX
David hasn't seen him either.

                    JULIET
So I gathered.

                    ALEX
Maybe he didn't like us.

                    JULIET
David?

                    ALEX
Hugo.

                    JULIET
His car's still there.

                    ALEX
He's got a car?

                    JULIET
So what's wrong with that?

ALEX

What sort of car?

JULIET

Alex, how would I know? I'm just a girl.

ALEX

I will ask you once more, what sort of car –

JULIET

A blue one, OK. And it's still there.

INT. HALL. NIGHT

We see the door to Hugo's room, then Alex rapping sharply against it.
David and Juliet stand behind him.

ALEX

Hugo. Hugo. Sorry about this, but can you open the door? It's us,
Hugo, your flatmates and companions. Your new-found friends.
He's not in. He's left and we'll probably never see him again.

JULIET

Alex, the key is in the keyhole on the other side.

ALEX

So?

JULIET

Open it.

ALEX

You want me to kick it open?

JULIET

Yes.

ALEX

Now?

JULIET

Yes.

ALEX

All right. No problem.

148

After a few rather ineffective kicks at the door, Alex turns to David.

You want a go?

INT. HUGO'S ROOM, NIGHT

Inside Hugo's room we see the door as David, outside, throws himself against it. At the third attempt the lock gives way and the door bursts open.

In the foreground at one side is the bed with a naked foot lying still and exposed.

When the door is open, David is first in, followed by the other two. There is a period of silent shock as they all contemplate Hugo's naked corpse. Alex opens a window.

DAVID

Is this what they always look like?

JULIET

Yes.

Juliet drapes a sheet over the body, covering it incompletely.

ALEX

I wonder how he did it?

JULIET

What?

ALEX

I wonder how he killed himself. I presume that that's what happened. What do you think?

Quite casually, Alex begins to open drawers and cupboards, emptying the contents on to the floor.

JULIET

Alex.

ALEX

What? What's wrong?

JULIET

What are you doing?

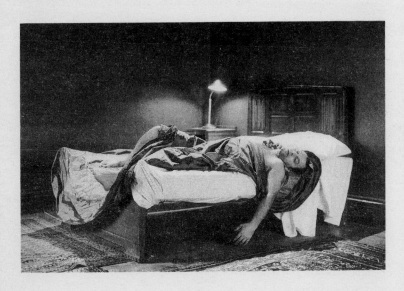

ALEX

I'm just looking.

JULIET

Don't.

ALEX

Don't look?

JULIET

No.

ALEX

Why not? What's wrong, Juliet? Aren't you curious? Don't you wonder what he died from?

JULIET

No. The guy's dead. What more do you need?

ALEX

It's not every day I find a story in my own flat.

JULIET

That's not a story, it's a corpse.

*[ALEX

Old newspaper proverb says dead human being is living story. Be rational, please, and failing that be quiet.]

In a drawer in a bedside cabinet, Alex finds needles, syringes and a small bag of white powder. Without comment, he holds it up and throws it on to the bed.

He reaches under the bed and pulls out a case, which he opens. It is empty and he pushes it back under.

DAVID

I've never seen a dead body before.

JULIET

Alex, I think it's about time for you to stop.

Alex continues to search. Juliet walks out.

*Cut from completed film.

INT. HALL. NIGHT

Juliet stands alone.

INT. HUGO'S ROOM. NIGHT

*Alex continues his brisk search through Hugo's possessions while David
looks on, appalled but speechless.*

INT. HALL. NIGHT

*Juliet listens to the sounds from the bedroom, then picks up the
telephone. She dials 999 and waits for a reply. It rings and rings.*

INT. HUGO'S ROOM, NIGHT.

*Alex has found and opened a large Gladstone bag. Neither David nor
we can see into it.*

DAVID

I saw my grandmother, of course, but I don't suppose that counts,
I mean, she was alive at the time.

ALEX

Can I show you something?

INT. HALL. NIGHT

Juliet awaits an answer.

*Alex approaches Juliet with the open bag. She turns around and looks
into it, then, seeing the contents, she replaces the receiver. As she does so,
the Operator's voice is audible for a second.*

OPERATOR

Hello, emergency services.

The telephone hits the cradle.

INT. KITCHEN. NIGHT

*David, Alex and Juliet are seated in silence around the table. The bag,
stacked with money, lies open on the table.*

DAVID

No.

ALEX

Think about it.

DAVID

No.

ALEX

Come on, David.

DAVID

No.

ALEX

Juliet?

JULIET

No, Alex. It's, it's –

ALEX

What?

JULIET

Unfeasible.

ALEX

Is that all?

DAVID

You mean immoral.

ALEX

I'm only asking you both to think about it.

DAVID

It's a sick idea, Alex. It's sick.

ALEX

But don't tell me that you're not tempted by it. Don't tell me that you're not interested. I know you well enough.

DAVID

You think so?

ALEX
(*amused*)

All right, then, go ahead, telephone. Telephone the police. Try
again. No one's going to stand in your way. Go ahead. Tell them
there's a suitcase of money and you don't want it.

They sit in silence.

INT. HALL. MORNING

*The flat is silent. Footsteps are heard outside the door and mail falls
through the letter box.*

INT. LIVING ROOM. DAY

The living room, empty.

INT. KITCHEN. DAY

The kitchen, empty. The bag of money still sits on the table.

INT. HUGO'S BEDROOM. DAY

*His corpse still lies on the bed, covered as before, incompletely, by a
sheet, with parts of his body still showing (a foot, a hand, part of his
face or abdomen).*

INT. NEWSPAPER OFFICE. DAY

*The open-plan office of a busy newspaper. Alex sits at his desk. He is
talking on a telephone jammed against his shoulder and while he does so
he is casually acknowledging and waving at colleagues.*

ALEX

Now, was there a pet in the house? Yes, a pet, like a dog or budgie
or a gerbil. You see, what I need is 'PC Plod rescues Harry the
Hamster from House of Horror'. All right . . . well, that's a pity,
you see, no pets, no human angle.

Alex hangs up.

INT. HUGO'S ROOM. DAY

Another view of the body: for example, from above.

INT. HOSPITAL. DAY

In the accident and emergency department of a busy hospital, Juliet sifts through a set of case notes. Another Doctor approaches her.

DOCTOR

Hi, there.

Juliet does not look up.

JULIET

Hello.

DOCTOR

What happened to that guy?

JULIET

What guy?

DOCTOR

That guy, that one that died.

Juliet looks up.

                              JULIET
What guy that died?

                              DOCTOR
That one, last week.

                              JULIET
Here?

                              DOCTOR
Yeah, here, I mean, where else?

                              JULIET
Oh, him. Well, he died.

                              DOCTOR
                            (*satisfied*)
That's what I thought.

INT. HUGO'S ROOM. DAY

*The body, still present, exposed and motionless. The curtain flutters by
the open window.*

INT. LUMSDEN'S OFFICE. DAY

*Lumsden, a middle-aged chartered accountant, is seated in a large chair
behind a desk. He is talking to David, who appears distracted.*

                            LUMSDEN
What do we do here, David?

                              DAVID
Sorry?

                            LUMSDEN
Here.

                              DAVID
Right here?

                            LUMSDEN
In this firm.

DAVID

Well, it's a wide range of, eh –

LUMSDEN

Accounting, David, chartered accounting –

DAVID

Exactly what I was –

LUMSDEN

– is often sneered at. Were you aware of that?

DAVID

Not any real sneering as such, no.

LUMSDEN

There's a whole wide world out there, and it all needs to be
accounted for, doesn't it?

DAVID

Eh –

LUMSDEN

But they sneer, don't they?

DAVID

I'm not sure –

LUMSDEN

Oh, it's unfashionable, I know, but, yes, we're methodical, yes,
we're diligent, yes, we're serious, and where's the crime in that,
and why not shout it from the rooftops, yes, maybe sometimes we
are a little bit boring, but by God, we get the job done.

DAVID

Yes, sir.

LUMSDEN

And that's why I think you fit in here.

DAVID

I'm boring?

LUMSDEN

You get the job done.

DAVID

Oh, I see, I thought you meant –

LUMSDEN

Which is why I'm trusting you with this account.

Lumsden throws a heavy folder into David's lap.

INT. HUGO'S ROOM. EVENING

It is almost dark. Only the familiar contour is visible through the gloom.

INT. STAIRWELL. EVENING

David ascends the stairs to the flat.

INT. LIVING ROOM. EVENING

Alex sits in an armchair facing out of the window. Juliet stands facing into the room. David, the last home, appears in the doorway.

DAVID

He's still here.

ALEX

He couldn't get his car started.

DAVID

When are you going to let the police know?

ALEX

You call them if you want.

DAVID
(*to Juliet*)

And what about you?

JULIET

Well, I'm getting used to having him around.

INT. HUGO'S ROOM. DAY

The corpse as before.

INT. ACCOUNTANTS' OFFICES. DAY

David sits at his desk, looking across the office.

Crouched over a large array of other desks, young men and women in suits are poring over folders and columned books. No one is speaking except in muted tones on the telephone.

David watches them. He looks to his left and to his right: on either side young men like him are toiling over accounts. He turns and looks behind him, where another array of accountants sit.

He turns back to his desk and opens the file he was previously given. He looks at the columns of records of profit, with a large total at the bottom.

When David looks up he sees Juliet seated beside his desk. She smiles and directs his gaze, with her own, to the surrounding scene.

INT. HUGO'S ROOM. EVENING

The body in silhouette.

> DAVID
> (*voice-over*)

OK. Let's do it.

INT. DIY STORE. DAY

Inside a large, brightly lit DIY store with Muzak playing in the background. We start with a tracking shot along an aisle stacked with potentially vicious tools.

> ALEX
> (*voice-over*)

All right, now listen. We have to dispose of that body in such a way as to make it unidentifiable, so that even if it is found, then it's never anything more than an unknown corpse. Burning, dumping at sea and straightforward burial are all flawed either by fingerprints or, more commonly, by dental records. This I have learned. Now, what I suggest is that we bury him out in the forest, but first of all we remove his hands and his feet, which we incinerate. And his teeth, which we just remove. It's as simple as that.

> *As the tracking shot ends, we see David's head and shoulders as he looks at something off picture. Suddenly a spring-loaded screwdriver appears and is 'fired' so that the tip stops a few millimetres from his face. David winces as we see that Alex is holding it.*

I always wondered what these were for.

> *Alex places the screwdriver down on the shelf and walks across the aisle to pick up a saw and a hammer.*

Now, this is what we need. And this.

> *Alex hands the tools to David, who looks at them with disgust. Alex walks on.*

Now what else?

> DAVID

I don't know.

> ALEX

A spade, we need a spade – I wish you would concentrate – we need a spade if we're going to dig a pit.

> DAVID

So who's going to do it?

ALEX

Dig the pit, I don't know.

DAVID

No, not that.

ALEX

Then what? Who's going to do what?

DAVID

You know what I'm talking about.

ALEX

Do I? What? What? What are you talking about?

DAVID

You know what. Who's going to do it?

ALEX

We all are, David, we're all going to do it. Each of us, you, me and Juliet, will do his or her bit. Is that fair enough?

DAVID

I can't do it.

ALEX

I don't hear this.

DAVID

I won't be able to do it.

ALEX

You're telling me you want out? Already? You're telling me you don't want the money? Hugo is going off. He smells. The flat smells. We can't wait any longer.

DAVID

I'm just telling you I can't cut him up.

Alex turns away in disgust.

EXT. LANE. NIGHT

Late at night, in a quiet lane at the back of the flat, a hired Ford Transit is parked.

161

INT. VAN. NIGHT

Inside the dimly lit van, Alex and Juliet are laying down plastic on the floor.

JULIET

Who's going to do it?

ALEX

I thought we all were.

JULIET

I don't think I can.

ALEX

But you're a doctor. You kill people every day.

JULIET

I still don't want to. It's different.

ALEX

And now you tell me.

INT. UNDER WATER/BATHROOM. NIGHT

A Man's face is being held under water. Bubbles escape from his mouth and his eyes bulge.

Tim hauls the Man's head out of the bath. His legs and arms are bound with cord. Andy sits on a chair, watching.

Tim ducks the Man's head under the water again.

The Man's face as before.

INT. HUGO'S ROOM. NIGHT

We see Hugo's face just before Alex, David and Juliet wrap him in a sheet and thick, black plastic. They wear masks over their noses. The smell is making them uncomfortable and irritable.

DAVID

There's something I want to ask.

INT. BATHROOM. NIGHT

The Man's head has just been lifted from the water.

                              MAN
I don't know. I swear to God, I don't know.

Tim ducks the Man's head back under the water.

INT. HUGO'S ROOM. NIGHT

                             ALEX
                    (*angry through his mask*)
Family? Family? Friends? Drugged-up wandering suicidal search
of the self fuck-ups don't have families, David.

                             DAVID
I just thought we sould discuss it.

                             ALEX
Take his legs.

INT. STAIRWELL. NIGHT

*In the stairwell of the flat, grunts of effort are heard as Alex, David and
Juliet struggle with the heavy corpse, carrying it down the stairs
wrapped in plastic sheeting. They come into view and go on down the
stairs. They are all very tense and freeze with panic after accidentally
banging against another flat's door. They swear at one another and
continue their descent.*

INT. BATHROOM. NIGHT

*Tim is ducking the Man again. He writhes and struggles but is
powerless to stop it.*

EXT. BEHIND THE FLAT. NIGHT

*The back yard and back door of the flats. The door opens and Alex,
David and Juliet emerge, carrying the corpse out towards the van.*

INT. LANDING OUTSIDE THE BATHROOM. NIGHT

From the landing we can see along the floor into the bathroom. The

Man's legs extend away from the bath. They are completely still. Andy and Tim stand beside them, looking down.

ANDY

You stupid bastard.

INT. VAN. NIGHT

Inside the back of the empty van. The door is opened and the body is half slid and half thrown inside. The door is closed and in the dark interior, the outline of the plastic lump is just visible, thanks to a streetlight. One of the doors opens again and David throws a bag of tools in. He then closes and locks the door.

INT. VAN. NIGHT

In the front of the van, David is climbing into the passenger side. Juliet and Alex are already in, with the latter at the wheel. Alex turns to the other two.

ALEX

Why don't we just draw lots for it?

The other two remain silent.

Whoever draws the short straw does it all. That way, you either do it or you don't. All or nothing.

JULIET

OK.

ALEX

David?

DAVID

I don't know.

ALEX

Look, if I draw the short straw, then I'll do it, but I'm not going to do it just because you won't.

Alex starts the engine of the van.

EXT. FOREST. NIGHT

Through the darkness we hear an engine, then the headlights of the van come into view.

It pulls off the track on to a patch of grass. The engine is switched off but the lights remain on. The trio descend from the van.

In front of the van, illuminated by its lights, Alex, David and Juliet stand together. Alex is showing them two long stems of grass and one short one. He encloses them in his fist and holds them out.

ALEX

All right, then, here we are and this is it. Do you want to play or not?

Alex holds his hand out towards Juliet, who takes the tip of one of the stems. It is one of the longer ones.

Alex and Juliet turn to David. Alex holds out the stems. David reaches out and takes one of the tips. It is the short straw.

DAVID

I can't do it.

EXT. FOREST. NIGHT

Deeper in the forest, with the headlamps still casting a little light through the trees, we see David's head and shoulders. His right arm is moving briskly back and forth accompanied by a vicious sawing noise. The sawing stops as he has evidently finished with one extremity. He shuffles back and starts sawing at another.

Alex leans against the spade in a shallow pit that he has dug. He observes David impassively. The sawing stops again.

DAVID

Finished.

ALEX

But not quite.

DAVID
(*hoping to distract Alex*)

Is that going to be deep enough?

Alex bends down to pick up the hammer, which he holds out towards David.

ALEX

Don't you worry about that.

JULIET

Is this necessary?

ALEX

Yes. Now come on, all or nothing.

Most reluctantly, David takes the hammer and looks at Alex, who gestures as if to say, 'On you go.' With revulsion on his face, he raises the hammer above his head.

INT. DAVID'S ROOM. DAY

David's face is visible against the plain white backdrop of his pillow.

He lies fully clothed on his bed, looking up at the ceiling. There is a knock at the door, then Juliet walks in.

JULIET

Are you all right?

DAVID
(*without looking at Juliet*)
Oh, yes, I'm fine, thanks, just fine.

JULIET

Would you like to talk about it?

DAVID

No.

INT. LIVING ROOM. DAY

Alex sits with his feet up watching a noisy game show, while eating a snack and drinking from a can of beer. Newspapers lie scattered at his feet.

INT. LOFT. DAY

The loft above the flat is in darkness, but the trapdoor is opened, letting in a pool of light.

INT. HALL. DAY

David is pulling himself through the trapdoor up into the loft. Beneath him is a stepladder. Juliet stands half-way up the ladder, while Alex stands on the floor beside it. As David enters the loft, Alex hands up the bag of money to Juliet, who passes it on up to David.

JULIET

Be careful.

ALEX

Yeah, we don't want another stiff on our hands. Don't fall through the ceiling. OK? Is he listening to me?

JULIET

Stop nagging.

ALEX
(to himself)

I don't know why we couldn't stuff it in a mattress or put it under the floor like any normal human being. We could have hid it in the fridge.

INT. LOFT. DAY

David moves on into the dark cavernous loft, edging his way across beams and pipes. There are no skylights.

He stops and leans against some structure (the water tank). He strains to see in the darkness.

Suddenly there is a loud sucking and flowing noise as water empties from the water tank. David is startled and steps forward, tripping. He reaches out as he falls, striking a light switch. Briefly the loft is illuminated: David blinking as he lies across some beams, the large cavernous area, the pipes, the water tank, the bag of money lying between two rafters, and then the old brass switches begin to spark and the light goes out.

David scrambles towards the trapdoor.

INT. HUGO'S ROOM. DAY

Now cleaned and empty, with no trace of recent habitation.

INT. HOSPITAL. DAY

In a basement corridor in the hospital, pipes run along the ceiling. Above a fenced-off area is a sign saying 'For Incineration Only – No Aerosols'. On the floor of this area are yellow plastic sacks. Juliet appears around a corner carrying one of these. Quite casually she dumps it on the pile and continues past.

EXT. QUARRY. EVENING

Alex pushes a blue car into a quarry.

**[INT. SUBURBAN LOCK-UP GARAGE. NIGHT

In the garage there is a car, gardening equipment, several sacks of fertilizer and a trunk-style deep freeze, on the lid of which sit Andy and Tim. Tim takes out a cigarette and offers one to Andy, who declines.

They slide off the deep freeze and open it.

Inside the freezer there is a man, naked and bound with cord. They lift him up. He is very cold and weak.

The Man begins to whisper inaudibly. Andy moves his head so that he can hear the whisper. He listens, then nods approvingly.

They push him down again and close the lid. Andy holds the lid while Tim dumps the sacks of fertilizer on top.]

INT. CHARITY BALL. NIGHT

Alex, David and Juliet are attending a charity ball. Everyone is dressed very smartly, in ball gowns and black ties with the addition of a significant number in kilts.

Neither Alex nor David wears a kilt. The trio seem to know a number of people there but do not seem especially keen to speak to them.

A middle-aged, podgy, mustachioed Master of Ceremonies is standing on a platform in front of the band, making a speech to the diners who are still sat at their tables.

**Scene used later in final film.

MC

Ladies and gentlemen, may I have your attention please. First of all, may I thank you all for coming along tonight and supporting our appeal to raise funds for the sick children's unit.

There is a quick drum roll and applause breaks out. We move to the table where Alex, David and Juliet are seated. Alex leans across to Juliet.

ALEX

You didn't tell me that this was for children. I hate children. I'd raise money to have the little fuckers put down.

Some other guests around the table cast critical glances at Alex.

JULIET

Sshh.

ALEX

I want my money back. Excuse me.

Alex signals to the waiter by lifting his hand and snapping his fingers, then indicates another bottle of the champagne that already sits in front of him.

MC

For all too often there's a complacency: out of sight, out of mind, let someone else bother about these things.

Alex cheers once and starts to applaud on his own. Juliet nudges him viciously.

But just before the dancing, I'd like to say a special thank-you to a few of the people who've worked so very hard to make this occasion actually happen.

The MC's drone continues in the background while conversation continues back at the table.

DAVID

Do you know many of these people?

JULIET

Yes. They're my friends.

ALEX

I see, so if they want to talk to you, we say you're not in.

MC

And now, ladies and gentlemen, and those of you who are neither or both –

Drum roll.

– would you make your way to the floor for the Strip the Willow.

JULIET

Are we going to dance?

ALEX

Well, it's physical contact, isn't it?

INT. DANCE FLOOR. NIGHT

The dance floor a few minutes later. It is packed and rather chaotic. Sweaty, dishevelled dancers sling one another around, with the thud of flesh against flesh. Toes are stood on and jackets discarded.

Juliet dances with Alex, who plunges in with the maximum of violence, eventually tripping up and tumbling forcefully among the other dancers.

172

He starts to get up, then rests his head back against the floor.

David has not been dancing. Instead he remains at their table and at the bar, drinking steadily and watching the other two.

INT. TABLE. NIGHT

Back at the table, while most people are still on the dance floor, the trio sit drinking and Alex smokes a cigar.

ALEX

That was good.

DAVID

Can we talk about something?

ALEX

Not now. I have an idea.

Alex pours champagne on to a stack of glasses.

DAVID

Listen, it's important. We need to talk about what we're going to do –

ALEX

Just stop worrying.

Alex stands and raises his glass.

Love and happiness for ever.

JULIET

For ever and ever.

Alex drinks, then puts his glass down. Juliet drinks but does not drain her glass. David sits still.

ALEX

What's the problem?

DAVID

I want to talk now.

ALEX

After you drink to love and happiness for ever.

Now.

ALEX

After.

JULIET

David, I promise we will. Keep him happy.

ALEX

It's not for me, it's for love and happiness for ever.

*David reaches out to take his glass. Suddenly Alex flings an arm out
to point, knocking over David's glass and completely losing interest.*

Look over there. It's Cameron.

JULIET

Who?

ALEX

Cameron. You remember Cameron.

JULIET

No, I don't.

ALEX

What's he doing here?

JULIET

That's not him.

ALEX

Yes, it is. It's him. Cameron, Cameron, come on over. Yo!

*From some distance away, Cameron becomes aware of Alex and
cautiously makes his way across until he stands a few feet from the table.*

CAMERON

What?

ALEX

Nothing. We thought you were someone else.

*Alex falls forwards, laughing, and the other two also laugh as
Cameron walks away, humiliated again.*

Good luck. I love that guy, but why does he have to follow us around?

DAVID

Anyway, what I was wanting to say was this –

BRIAN
(*unseen*)

The divine Juliet. Long time no see.

Brian has approached and is standing behind their table.

JULIET

Brian.

BRIAN

Would you care to dance?

DAVID

Hold on there. Who do you think you are?

BRIAN

What?

DAVID

Who do you think you are? You interrupted us.

BRIAN

I'm Brian McKinley, and who are you?

DAVID

Well, Brian McKinley, if you want to talk to my girlfriend, you talk to me first. If you want to dance with her, then you apply in writing three weeks in advance or you're gonna end up inside a fucking bin-bag. You didn't apply, so you don't dance.

Shocked and frightened, Brian backs away, then turns around to complete his departure. Juliet restrains David with a touch as they watch him go.

JULIET

Do you think you could try to be a little more forceful next time?

DAVID

I'm sorry.

JULIET

It's all right. I think he got the message anyway.

DAVID

That was quite stressful. I found that stressful.

ALEX

Yeah, but you were good, you were really good. 'Fucking bin-bag', I liked that. You were good. You explored your maleness to the full there.

DAVID

Do you think so?

JULIET

Well, you certainly had a good look around.

ALEX

You were magnificent.

INT. TOILETS. NIGHT

The gents' toilets. Brightly lit and white-tiled. Alex walks in and goes into a cubicle and closes the door. We hear him whistling and laughing as he passes urine. He keeps muttering 'bin-bag' to himself. Then he flushes the toilet and opens the door. As he does so a look of surprise appears on his face as he sees someone waiting for him.

ALEX

Cameron! What a surprise.

As Alex is speaking Cameron's fist flies forward, hitting him in the face and sending him flying backwards. Cameron enters the cubicle and closes the door behind him.

INT. KITCHEN. MORNING

Juliet sits as before at the table. Alex sits opposite her, in his dressing gown. He looks vacant and unhappy, and there is bruising on his face. The newspapers are unread in a neat pile.

INT. HALL. MORNING

Mail falls through the letter box.

INT. KITCHEN. MORNING

Alex does not stir.

INT. HALL. MORNING

David emerges from his room, ready for work. He looks towards the kitchen, then walks to the door and opens it.

INT. KITCHEN. MORNING

We hear the main door closing as David leaves. Alex jolts with every sound. The telephone begins to ring. Juliet looks at Alex expectantly, but he does not move. Eventually she gets up and answers it.

> JULIET
Hello. Hello.

> ALEX
Who was it?

> JULIET
Don't know. No one said anything.

> ALEX
Rendered speechless with desire. I recall that feeling, from the days when I had such a thing.

> JULIET
Are you all right?

> ALEX
No.

> JULIET
Then let's spend some money.

INT. FLAT. DAY

There follows a video depicting the results of Alex's and Juliet's spending spree. It opens with Alex seated at the kitchen table talking to the camera, absolutely deadpan.

> ALEX
Hello. It's been a struggle, but now the days of worry are over, the

178

light at the end of the tunnel has expanded into a golden sunrise and at last, at long last, nothing will ever be the same again.

Alex leans out and the camera follows him as he presses the play button on a tape recorder. The music begins.

Fast cuts follow, occasionally interrupted by out-of-focus shots of the floor or ceiling as the camera swivels round and is switched on and off.

Alex wearing several different suits, outfits and silk pyjamas.

Juliet wearing several different outfits.

Both of them posing with small objets d'art.

The expensive watch on Alex's wrist.

Juliet's jewellery.

Expensive toys.

Juliet takes a picture of Alex with a Polaroid camera.

Alex holds the camcorder out at arm's length in order to film himself and turns to the camera and adjusts his tie.

This is Alex Law reporting from the scene of his own life, and you know, I'm so happy I could die.

Darkness. TV. Turned off.

INT. LIVING ROOM. DAY

The music has stopped.

David presses the eject button and lifts the video from the player.

Alex and Juliet are seated on the sofa, surrounded by their acquisitions, and are evidently a little embarrassed. Juliet is holding the Polaroid of Alex.

DAVID

I think we ought to scrub this, don't you?

David reinserts the tape and presses record.

Will you calm down.

Yeah, you're making us all nervous.

David picks up the Polaroid of Alex and throws it down, then picks up a vase.

DAVID
How much did you pay for this?

ALEX
I don't know.

DAVID
How much did you pay?

ALEX
I don't know.

DAVID
How much?

ALEX
I don't know.

JULIET
Two hundred.

DAVID
Two hundred pounds?

JULIET
Two hundred pounds.

DAVID
You paid two hundred pounds for this?

JULIET
That's what it cost, David.

DAVID
No, no, no. That's what you paid for it. Two hundred pounds is what you paid for it. We don't know what it cost us yet, for you two to have a good time, we don't know the cost of that yet.

From out in the hall, the telephone starts to ring. Nobody moves.

INT. DAVID'S ROOM. NIGHT

David lies awake in his bed.

INT. A FLAT HALLWAY. NIGHT

In a dark hallway, a door is kicked forcefully open.

INT. DAVID'S ROOM. NIGHT

Hearing the noise, David sits up in bed, then gets out, reaching for his clothes.

INT. STAIRWELL. NIGHT

David looks down the stairwell. Other neighbours, in nightclothes or hurriedly dressed, are standing at the open door of the flat below. David descends the stairs and looks into the hall of the other flat where the occupant, an Elderly Woman, lies groaning on the floor.

A hand on David's shoulder pushes him out of the way and two uniformed policemen walk past, followed by ambulance men carrying a stretcher.

DAVID

Did they take anything? Did they take anything?

No one acknowledges his question or answers it.

The ambulance men emerge carrying the woman, her face bruised and cut. Everyone else begins to melt away.

INT. STAIRWELL. NIGHT

David stands alone on the darkened stairwell.

INT. DAVID'S ROOM. NIGHT

David lies awake in his bed.

*[INT. DOOR OF THE FLAT. DAY

Someone attempts to open the door but cannot because there are two new security chains on the inside. The door is forced against the chains with no success and Alex calls out from the other side.

ALEX

What is this? What is going on? David!

David approaches the door.

DAVID

I'll let you in.

David closes the door and looks through a new spyhole to see Alex grinning at him while he releases the chains and then opens the door again. Alex walks in.

ALEX

What is this?

DAVID

Security.

ALEX

For what? Jehovah's Witnesses?

DAVID

There was a break-in.

ALEX

Downstairs, I know. Pensioner's terror ordeal: page six.

Alex hands David a rolled-up newspaper.

DAVID

Doesn't it worry you?

ALEX

No, it doesn't. I've tried to let it worry me but it won't. I've worked on that paper for three years. There is a pensioner's terror ordeal on page six every day. Every day. Maybe when I'm a pensioner it'll worry me.

*Cut from completed film.

Alex notices some more tools and the stepladder leading up to the trapdoor.

What's all this for, more security?

DAVID

I fitted a lock up there. On the inside.

ALEX

Oh, that'll come in useful.]

INT. KITCHEN. NIGHT

Alex is serving on to plates from a large bowl of pasta.

David and Juliet sit at the table.

*[JULIET

Is this the same stuff you made last week?

ALEX

No, no, it's different.

JULIET

I hope it tastes better than the other stuff.

ALEX

It tastes different.

JULIET

I don't want it to taste different. I don't know why I bother.] Is that enough for you? Hey!

DAVID

What? Yes, that's fine.

ALEX

You're sure? There's lots more.

DAVID

No, I'm sure, that'll be enough.

ALEX

What's wrong?

*Cut from completed film.

183

DAVID

Nothing.

ALEX

You're not eating.

DAVID

Not eating what?

ALEX

Not eating like you used to, that's what.

DAVID

If you give me the plate, I'll eat.

Alex hands him the plate and he starts to eat. Alex watches him chew a mouthful.

ALEX

Now swallow.

David does so.

You know, you should spend some of that money instead of worrying about it. That's my advice.

JULIET

He's right. You'd feel much better about it all.

David has stopped eating.

ALEX

Once it's spent you won't have to worry about it.

JULIET

Be like a weight off your shoulders.

ALEX

You know we're right.

JULIET

Don't you?

DAVID

I want to secure it.

ALEX

Secure it? What do you mean – you're going to take it to a bank?
You're not going to take it to a bank? You're not going to take it to
a bank? Or what, you want to bury it? Is that it?

JULIET

I don't see the point in that.

ALEX

Because that's no good. Remember, we did what we did, we took
the money. It was a material calculation. But what's the use if it's
underground, or in some funny bank in some funny place? If you
can't spend it, if you can't have it, what use is it? None. It's
nothing, all for nothing, if you do that. I didn't get into this for
nothing, so that I could have nothing –

DAVID

Yeah, and you didn't saw his feet off.

There is silence. David resumes eating.

It tastes different.

INT. HALL. NIGHT.

The trapdoor is closed and we hear the lock turning.

INT. KITCHEN. NIGHT.

*Alex stands at the sink doing some washing up. He hears footsteps from
the loft above. He stops what he is doing and walks slowly out to the
hall.*

INT. LOFT. NIGHT

In the darkness we can just make out David's eyes as he sits in silence.

ALEX
(*calling from below*)

David, David, what are you doing up there?

*The torch goes on. David lifts the bag of money from between the
rafters. He puts it inside another thick yellow plastic bag, which he
ties tightly with string.*

David then opens the water tank.

Alex's voice can be heard throughout.

(*calling from below*)

Will you come down now. It's not safe up there. Are you listening to me? Security and insanity are not the same thing.

INT. HALL. NIGHT

ALEX

Shit.

*[INT. KITCHEN. MORNING

Juliet sits drinking coffee, while Alex stands in the doorway looking up towards the trapdoor.

JULIET

Leave him alone.

ALEX

He can't stay up there.

JULIET

He'll come down. Just leave him alone.

ALEX

Yeah, he's got to go to work, hasn't he? You think he'll come down for that?

JULIET

No, but he's looking after the money, so what's the problem?

ALEX

Looking after it – he's probably fucking well eating it.]

*[INT. HOSPITAL. DAY

Juliet looks through the door from a small office out into the main waiting area in the casualty department. It is busy and there are rows of people nursing injuries waiting to be seen. More file past the door while she watches with no enthusiasm.]

*Cut from completed film.

INT. HALL. DAY

The trapdoor opens. David's head appears. He looks around and listens carefully.

INT. LUMSDEN'S OFFICE. DAY

Lumsden answers his telephone.

INT. HALL. DAY

David speaks on the telephone.

DAVID

It's my mother, sir, she's very ill and I think I need to be with her just now. I don't know. The doctors aren't sure. It could go either way. Yes, sir, I'll certainly stay in touch.

INT. BATHROOM. DAY

David shaves carefully with a safety razor.

*[INT. KITCHEN. DAY

Bacon and eggs fry in a pan. David attends to them while drinking from a large tumbler of orange juice.

INT. HOSPITAL. DAY

A Sister hands Juliet a casualty case sheet. Juliet reads it.

JULIET

Painful groin? What does that mean?

SISTER

I don't know. He wouldn't show me.]

Juliet draws back the curtain of a cubicle. Alex is sitting on a trolley.

*[ALEX

Boy, am I glad to see you.

*Cut from completed film.

JULIET

What are you doing here?

ALEX

We have to talk.

JULIET

Your painful groin?

She turns and walks away. Alex chases after her.

ALEX

Later. But first – him.]

JULIET

David?

ALEX

Exactly. Now I've been thinking –

JULIET

Oh, good.

ALEX

He won't do anything for me, but for you –

JULIET

Forget it.

ALEX

He isn't safe up there. If you really cared about him, you'd use your influence to get him down, then he'd be safe.

JULIET

And the money?

ALEX

We could put it somewhere.

JULIET

Where he can't get it?

ALEX

Now you thought of that, not me.

JULIET

Forget it – he'll come down.

Juliet walks away.

INT. HALL. DAY

The hall is empty and the flat is silent. We see the trapdoor.

INT. LOFT. EVENING

David sits in the darkness. A crack of light penetrates beside the trapdoor.

INT. KITCHEN. NIGHT

Alex and Juliet sit at the table, eating in silence.

The doorbell rings. Alex and Juliet look at one another.

ALEX

Expecting anyone?

JULIET

No.

ALEX

Oh.

Alex resumes eating.

JULIET

Aren't you going to answer it?

ALEX

Well, I'm not expecting anyone either.

Juliet glares at him.

INT. HALL. NIGHT

Alex approaches the door and is about to open it. At the last moment he checks himself and looks through the spyhole.

INT. THROUGH THE SPYHOLE. NIGHT

Tim and Andy stand outside the door.

INT. HALL. NIGHT

Alex, slightly puzzled, fixes the security chains before opening the door. As soon as he opens it, the door is kicked wide open as the security chains break off. Tim and Andy enter the flat.

In a whirlwind of force they drag and shove Alex and Juliet into the living room and bind them up with cord. There are no words apart from swiftly muffled cries.

At the end of this Andy stands in front of Alex holding a crowbar. Swiftly and without warning, he cracks it across Alex's shins. Then Andy slowly puts one end of the crowbar into Alex's mouth. For a moment he does nothing, then just as slowly again, he takes the crowbar out.

ALEX

It's in the loft.

INT. HALL. NIGHT

The trapdoor is closed but the sound of it being unlocked can just be heard (although not by anyone in the flat).

INT. HALL. NIGHT

Tim pulls the ladder across to the trapdoor.

INT. LOFT. NIGHT

It is completely dark in the loft, but as the trapdoor opens a shaft of light strikes upwards and illuminates a small pool around the opening.

INT. LOFT. NIGHT

Away from the trapdoor there appears to be a wall of uniform darkness, but then we see a pair of eyes in the darkness. It is David. He stands perfectly still.

There is a hammer in his right hand.

INT. LOFT. NIGHT

Tim's head appears through the trapdoor. Cautiously he lifts himself through and balances on the beams.

INT. HALL. NIGHT

The hall is empty, but we can see the open trapdoor. Suddenly there is a single thud, as might be caused by a body landing heavily on and across some beams in the loft.

INT. LOFT. NIGHT

David stands motionless in the dark, exactly as before.

INT. LIVING ROOM. NIGHT

Andy has heard the single thud. He strains to hear anything else but does not. Slowly he backs away to the door of the living room, keeping the crowbar trained on Alex as he does so. He looks back and up towards the trapdoor.

INT. LOFT. NIGHT

Once again a small pool of light emanates from the open trapdoor. Andy emerges into this, crowbar in hand, peering into the darkness. Carefully he stands up and moves out of the light and steps across the beams. His foot strikes something and he looks down. Tim's body lies spread-eagled beneath him. He looks up. To one side of him is the brass light switch. Andy lifts his arm, reaches towards it and switches it on. Sparks pour out for a moment and then the light comes on for a fraction of a second, long enough for Andy to see David's face is only centimetres from his own.

INT. HALL. NIGHT

Alex and Juliet are bound together as before. There is a loud thud from the ceiling, followed by a few heavy steps. Then Andy's body falls headfirst through the trapdoor, straight down to the floor below, landing awkwardly and coming to rest with his head hanging back, looking towards Alex and Juliet. Andy takes one agonal breath and dies. Blood trickles from the side of his mouth.

Tim's body lands on Andy.

David drops himself from the hatch to the floor.

David takes a large knife from a wooden block.

Back in the hall he kneels, holding the knife, beside Tim. Noticing something at the top of Tim's neck, he uses the knife to lift away Tim's T-shirt. A tattoo covers Tim's neck. David looks at it, then stands up.

He walks through to the living room, where Alex and Juliet, still bound, watch him approach. He looks at them for a moment, then extends the knife and cuts the cord in one place.

EXT. FOREST. NIGHT

In a scene similar to the dismemberment of Hugo, we see David's shoulders as he saws back and forth at something unseen. He stops and reaches out for the hammer, picks it up and raises it above his head.

EXT. ROAD. DAWN

The van is silhouetted against a rising sun.

INT. BACK OF THE VAN. DAWN

The tools and the yellow sack slide about in the back of the van.

INT. VAN. DAWN

David is driving. Alex and Juliet are huddled silently away from him. David seems quite at ease.

A thick bunch of keys dangles from the ignition. Juliet observes them.

INT. LOFT. DAY

David sits still in the darkness.

*[INT. NEWSPAPER OFFICE. DAY

Alex sits at his desk fidgeting, about to write something but unable to start. On the screen of his word processor is a page mock-up with the

*Cut from completed film.

192

*headline 'CATS EAT PENSIONER'. As the telephone on his desk
rings, he is startled, then reaches out, slowly lifts it fractionally and
replaces it.*]

INT. TRAVEL AGENT'S. DAY

Hunched over a VDU, the Salesman is offering Juliet a range of flights.

SALESMAN
October 15th, direct flight, London Heathrow to Rio de Janeiro,
British Airways, you are looking at seven hundred and sixty-five
pounds. Seven six five.

JULIET
That sounds fine.

SALESMAN
Air Portugal, on the other hand, via Lisbon, same day, five
hundred and sixty-five. Five six five. It's up to you. Catering
important?

JULIET
What?

SALESMAN
Air France. Glasgow. Direct, but then you're looking at the wrong
end of nine hundred and twelve pounds. That's nine one two. It's
up to you.

JULIET
Yes, the first one's fine. Heathrow direct.

SALESMAN
It's up to you. Air Patagonia. New outfit: via Caracas and Bogotá.
No catering. Four hundred and eleven pounds. Four one one.
Good value, but refuelling at Bogotá is variable.

JULIET
The first one was fine.

SALESMAN
Well, it's up to you. Seven six five. How will you be paying?

INT. HALL. NIGHT

The hall is empty but we can hear David's footsteps on the beams above.

INT. LIVING ROOM. NIGHT

Alex sits watching The Wicker Man *on television. He can hear the footsteps above. He turns the sound up on the television so that he cannot hear them, but he keeps looking up to the ceiling, as though he expects to hear them or to see something.*

Eventually he turns the sound back down and, after a moment's silence, the footsteps start again, back and forth, then stop.

Alex looks up.

Without warning there is the sound of an electric drill.

The blade of the drill appears through the ceiling and is then withdrawn. Alex is shocked. Other drill holes appear.

INT. VARIOUS CEILINGS. NIGHT

Holes are drilled in the ceilings.

INT. LOFT. NIGHT

Rods of light penetrate up from the holes, interrupting but not obliterating the darkness. David sits back, pleased with his work.

INT. JULIET'S ROOM. NIGHT

Juliet sits at her desk. Alex stands in the doorway. He is about to speak. Juliet raises a finger to her lips. They both look at the ceiling.

EXT. GARDEN AT FRONT OF THE FLAT. NIGHT

Establishing shot of Alex and Juliet in garden.

INT. HALL. NIGHT

The trapdoor is open.

INT. ALEX'S ROOM. NIGHT

David is searching through Alex's desk, looking through letters and folders, then shoving them back into drawers.

EXT. GARDEN AT FRONT OF THE FLAT. NIGHT

                    ALEX
No, definitely not. And that's that. I refuse to discuss it further.

                    JULIET
It's the only way.

                    ALEX
I refuse.

                    JULIET
You're frightened.

                    ALEX
No, I'm not frightened. A little terrified maybe. Did you see what happened to the last two who tried that. They went up alive and they came down dead – the difference, I mean, alive dead dead alive, that sort of thing. It wasn't difficult to spot. He killed them both: he cut them up.

INT. JULIET'S ROOM. NIGHT

David is now searching through Juliet's desk. He picks up a large brown envelope and looks into it. Beneath it is the airline ticket envelope.

The doorbell rings.

INT. THROUGH THE SPYHOLE. NIGHT

McCall and Mitchell stand outside the door.

INT. HALL. NIGHT

David opens the door. McCall smiles.

197

MCCALL

Good evening. I'm Detective Inspector McCall and this is DC
Mitchell. I wonder if we could ask you some questions.

DAVID

What about?

MCCALL

It's about the burglary.

DAVID

Burglary?

MCCALL

Downstairs.

DAVID

Of course.

MCCALL

Can we come in?

INT. LIVING ROOM. NIGHT

*David sits on the sofa while the two policemen sit on armchairs several
feet apart.*

DAVID

So I just heard her cries for help and all that, and when I went
downstairs there were already those other people there, so I just
stood around really, waiting – you know how people do – and then
when your colleagues arrived I came back upstairs. And that's
about all, I think. I didn't actually see anything useful, I don't
think.

MCCALL

Did you hear anything before her cries?

DAVID

No, not that I recall. I was asleep.

MCCALL

Have you seen anything or anyone suspicious around here in the
last few days?

DAVID

No, nothing, sorry.

MCCALL

Well, if you do, you'll let us know?

DAVID

Of course.

MCCALL

And the other three people in the flat, did they hear anything?

DAVID

There are only two other people in the flat.

McCall consults a notebook.

MCCALL

Two?

DAVID

Who said there were four?

MCCALL

We understood there were four people living here. Not always, of course, but now, four.

DAVID

No, three. Who said there were four?

MCCALL

How strange. And how unsatisfactory to have misleading information. Only three people here. You're sure?

DAVID

Yes, absolutely.

MCCALL

Take a note of that, Mitchell. Only three, rather than four. Write it down. You can use numbers or words, I have no preference. Which are you using?

MITCHELL

Both, sir.

MCCALL

Excellent. DC Mitchell is a rising star, Mr Stevens. Under my tutelage he will undoubtedly make the grade.

DAVID

I see.

MCCALL

I doubt it. *[And these other two people, did they hear anything?

DAVID

No, they were asleep. They didn't even wake up.

MCCALL

Yes. Why do you think you woke and they didn't?

DAVID

I don't know. Maybe I'm a lighter sleeper.]

Uncomfortably, David realizes that Mitchell has noted down even this last, trivial remark in a painful longhand and has underlined a short segment of it.

*[INT. HALL. NIGHT

In the hallway of the flat Mitchell stands at the open main door, waiting to leave. McCall is kneeling at the door to Hugo's room, tracing his finger down the broken lintel and lock. David looks on.

MCCALL

Looks like you had a break-in up here as well.

DAVID

Someone lost the key.

McCall gently pushes the door open and the light from the hall illuminates Hugo's room.

MCCALL

Is this where no one stays?

DAVID

Yeah, that's right, that's it.

*Cut from completed film.

David notices that Mitchell is writing this down.]

EXT. GARDEN AT FRONT OF THE FLAT. NIGHT

ALEX

You'll wait in the hall?

JULIET

I'll wait there.

ALEX

And if it sounds like I'm being killed, you'll phone the police, you'll tell them everything?

JULIET

Everything.

ALEX

Everything. Except maybe it was his idea and not mine in the first place. OK? That's important to me. I need to die misunderstood.

JULIET

Alex.

ALEX

What?

JULIET

As smart as you are, you'll need a little help.

She hands Alex a Yale key. Alex stares at it.

INT. LOFT. NIGHT

In the darkness, the sound of the lock being turned is heard.

INT. HALL. NIGHT

Alex stands at the top of the ladder, holding the key in the trapdoor lock.

ALEX

All right, David, what I'm going to do is, I'm going to open this lock and I'm going to come up, and what's important is that you remain calm.

There is one light on. Juliet stands at the bottom of the ladder.
Having opened the trapdoor, Alex stops and listens, but there is no
sound above his own breathing. Juliet throws up a torch, which he
catches. He switches it on. It shines, then goes out, and he knocks it
against the ladder, making it work again. Slowly he pushes the
trapdoor open.

INT. LOFT. NIGHT

The trapdoor opens. Below it, Alex crouches on the ladder, expecting
attack at any moment. He looks back down to Juliet, who returns his
gaze, then slowly he raises himself into the loft.

He turns around quickly, darting the torchlight around into corners and
squinting in the darkness, but he sees nothing.

The torch goes out. Cursing, he knocks it against a beam and it shines
again.

Slowly he moves further from the trapdoor into the centre of the loft,
still turning around and worried about what might be behind or above
him.

INT. HALL. NIGHT

Juliet stands waiting, braced for sound of conflict.

INT. LOFT. NIGHT

Alex is still looking but has relaxed a little, feeling less in danger. In one
corner he notices David's pile of loft-possessions and the mat on which
he has been sleeping. He moves towards it.

INT. HALL. NIGHT

Juliet stands, still waiting.

INT. LOFT. NIGHT

Alex stands in David's corner. With another sweep of the torch he can
still see nothing. He calls to Juliet.

ALEX

He isn't up here.

INT. HALL. NIGHT

A close-up of Juliet's face, just as David's hand slams across her mouth, gripping her tightly while his other hand clamps the back of her head. David's mouth is right up against her ear as he spits a warning into it.

DAVID

Tell him to look for the money.

Slowly, David relaxes his grip on Juliet.

JULIET

Look for the money.

INT. LOFT. NIGHT

Alex, quite cheerful now, is looking in the rafters.

ALEX

Don't worry. That's what I'm doing.

INT. HALL. NIGHT

David holds Juliet across her face again. She is terrified and does not struggle.

*[DAVID

Expecting anyone?

JULIET

What?

DAVID

Were you expecting anyone? Tonight?

JULIET

No.

DAVID

Visitors? Some friends maybe? Someone you talked to?

*Cut from completed film.

                    JULIET
No one. I promise.

                    DAVID
Who have you talked to?

                    JULIET
No one.

                    DAVID
If I think you're lying –]

INT. LOFT. NIGHT

Alex stands gazing around the loft.

                    ALEX
                (from the loft)
Well, it's not up here.

INT. HALL. NIGHT

David pulls Juliet to one side.

INT. LOFT. NIGHT

*Alex is about to descend when he notices the water tank. He walks over
and lifts the lid. His face breaks into a smile as he realizes what it holds.
He dips an arm into the tank, raises the yellow bag, then quickly lowers
it again. Alex steps back from the water tank.*

INT. HALL. NIGHT

*Alex appears at the top of the ladder. Without looking, he slides down as
quickly as he can, calling out as he does so.*

                    ALEX
Juliet, I have –

   *Alex reaches the base of the ladder. He turns around to find himself
   facing the blade of the battery-operated drill, held by David. Juliet
   stands off to one side.*

– a problem.

David holds the drill even closer until it is almost touching the centre of Alex's forehead and presses the 'trigger' to turn the blade slowly as he speaks.

Alex does not move at all.

DAVID

You looking for me?

ALEX

Looking for you? Yes.

DAVID

What for? What did you want? The money? Was that it?

ALEX

We just wanted to speak to you.

Alex's hands and sleeves are wet. A few drops of water fall from his fingertips. Unnoticed by the other two, he slowly wipes his hands on the back of his jeans.

DAVID

Who else have you just wanted to speak to? Maybe you thought they'd already got me.

The blade of the drill scrapes Alex's skin.

ALEX

Who?

DAVID

Your friends.

ALEX

I don't know what you're talking about.

JULIET

He doesn't know David.

David holds the drill back slightly while he thinks. It could go either way.

DAVID

Well, maybe you don't –

David lowers the drill and smiles.

I'm talking about the police.

INT. ALEX'S ROOM. DAY

Alex has just woken up. He rubs at his forehead. There is a nick in it, where the drill scratched. He rubs at it and examines the drop of blood on the end of his finger.

INT. DAVID'S POINT OF VIEW. ALEX'S ROOM. DAY

Looking down from a hole in the ceiling, we see into Alex's room, where he is getting dressed. As he finishes dressing he leaves his room.

INT. HALL. DAY

Alex leaves his room and enters the hall.

INT. LOFT. DAY

David scurries across the beams to look down through a hole above the hall.

INT. LOFT/HALL. DAY

Looking down on Alex as he leaves the flat and closes the door.

INT. LOFT. DAY

David scurries back across the beams to look down through another hole. He looks for several seconds.

NOTE *In the following sequence, Juliet's face is not seen until her comment on it.*

INT. JULIET'S ROOM. DAY

Juliet lies on her bed. She throws the covers back.

INT. LOFT. DAY.

David is still looking down through the hole.

INT. JULIET'S ROOM. DAY

Juliet moves around her room. She is wearing a large, baggy T-shirt.

INT. LOFT. DAY

David still watching.

INT. JULIET'S ROOM. DAY

Juliet's legs are seen as the T-shirt lands on the floor beside them.

INT. LOFT. DAY

David sits back suddenly, recoiling from this activity. He scrambles back across to his mat, where he sits back down and closes his eyes. Then he opens them and scrambles back to look down again.

INT. JULIET'S ROOM. DAY

The room is empty

The sound of the flat door closing is heard.

From David's point of view we see:

    INT. LOFT/HALL (EMPTY). DAY

    INT. LOFT/LIVING ROOM (EMPTY). DAY

    INT. LOFT/KITCHEN (EMPTY). DAY

INT. HALL. DAY

David's head appears beneath the trapdoor. He hangs from the hatch and drops down to the floor.

INT. BATHROOM. DAY

David showers.

INT. HALL. DAY

David emerges from the bathroom and walks towards the kitchen. We follow him in.

INT. KITCHEN. DAY

David takes orange juice out of the fridge and pours himself a glass. He sits at the table and looks briefly into a corner that we cannot see. The expression on his face does not change and his voice is impassive.

DAVID

I thought you'd gone to work.

JULIET
(unseen)

With a face like this?

INT. KITCHEN. DAY

Juliet's face. There are bruises across it where she was gripped by David.

INT. MONITOR SCREEN/NEWSPAPER OFFICE. DAY

In close-up we track along the following half-sentence: 'In the event of my death I want the following facts to be known: –'

The remainder of the screen is blank.

Alex sits at his desk, deciding what to type next on to the screen seen before. A young Office Boy approaches his desk.

BOY

The editor wants to see you.

INT. KITCHEN. DAY

David sits still while Juliet talks. She is now seated just behind him.

*[JULIET
I remember how things used to be here, and I see how they are now, and I don't know why it is. I don't know how we let you become like this. We were your friends and we should have looked after you.]

*Cut from completed film.

INT. EDITOR'S OFFICE. DAY

Alex sits nervously while the Editor sits on the side of his desk.

EDITOR

Out in the woods. Three bodies. Decomposed. Mutilated. Beyond recognition.

ALEX

I don't know anything about it.

EDITOR

Of course you don't know anything about it. If you knew anything about it, I wouldn't have to send you out there to cover it.

ALEX

Cover it?

EDITOR

That's right. This is your break.

ALEX

Cover it?

EDITOR

Well?

*[ALEX
But there's no –

EDITOR

Animals involved? I know, but you need a change. And besides, we're short.]

ALEX

I don't know.

EDITOR

Don't know what?

ALEX

Well, I've got this story, it's really good, I'm working on, that is good, I feel it could be big, it's this, eh, and it's, you know, it's incredible. Am I right, you did say 'beyond recognition'?

*Cut from completed film.

209

INT. KITCHEN. DAY

David and Juliet are seated as before.

DAVID

I'm sorry.

JULIET

I should hope so.

David turns towards her. He reaches out and softly touches her face.

DAVID

Maybe we can still sort everything out.

Juliet takes his hand.

JULIET

Well, we could always try.

They look at one another.

EXT. FOREST. DAY

Several police and unmarked vehicles, including one mobile 'incident room', stand on a rough track. Another car arrives at the end and is parked to one side. Alex steps out.

From where he stands, Alex can see towards the site of the burials. There are a few policemen, uniformed and plain-clothes, and a small knot of journalists, kept at bay by plastic tape draped from tree to tree. Mounds of earth mark the site of the exhumations.

Alex walks past the other journalists into the woods. He looks back towards the sight, then turns to look in the opposite direction. He finds himself at the edge of a golf course. From the green to the graves is hardly any distance.

To one side, Alex sees McCall and Mitchell, hunched in earnest discussion. Mitchell looks up briefly and catches Alex's eye.

INT. KITCHEN/HALL. DAY

The kitchen is empty. We track through the kitchen and out into the hall, stopping at the door to Juliet's room.

INT. JULIET'S ROOM. DAY

David and Juliet are seated on the bed. Among the junk on her bedside table is the Polaroid photograph of Alex, propped up against a tumbler. Juliet reaches out and turns it away before pulling David towards her.

INT. MOBILE INCIDENT ROOM. DAY

Several journalists sit close together on plastic chairs. Alex sits at the back, near the half-open door. At the other end, three police officers face them. They are a medium-ranking Uniformed Officer, and to one side of him Mitchell and then McCall, both of whom sit in silence.

UNIFORMED OFFICER

All right, ladies and gentlemen, the releasable and print-worthy facts of the day so far are as follows. Late yesterday afternoon, forestry workers came across one set of human remains lying in a grave which appeared to have been recently dug. Further excavation on our part has revealed two similar, deeper graves, again containing human remains.

Alex turns his head and looks out of the door towards the burial site, now enclosed in a plastic tent. He continues to stare at it.

While Alex is looking, the sound of laughter and Uniformed Officer's subsequent comments become muted and we hear the memory of a sound in Alex's head: it is the noise of the saw going back and forth across the victim's limbs.

As and when the corpses are removed, we will endeavour to ascertain the mode of death and duration of burial, as well as identification, which will of course be passed on to you after informing, where possible, the next of kin.

Alex discreetly stands up and slips out of the van.

EXT. FOREST. DAY

Alex walks away from the incident room towards his car. He breaks into a run for a few paces.

The noise of the sawing continues.

As he reaches his car, Alex fumbles in his pockets for his keys. He is
sweating and trembling. He drops his keys. As he bends down to pick
them up, his foot slips on the wet grass. He falls to his knees, his
forehead banging against the car door. He kneels for a moment,
gripping the keys, his head resting against the door.

The noise of the sawing stops.

From behind, the arm of a Police Constable reaches out and his hand
rests on Alex's shoulder.

Alex turns around to see the Constable looming over him.

CONSTABLE

Are you all right sir?

INT. MOBILE INCIDENT ROOM. DAY

The Uniformed Officer continues.

McCall is staring impassively at the empty chair by the door.

INT. ALEX'S CAR. DAY

Alex sits in his car, staring ahead. Eventually he puts the key in the
ignition.

EXT. STREET. NIGHT

The outside of the tenement.

INT. STAIRWELL. NIGHT

Alex ascends the stairs. He is carrying three copies of the next day's
edition.

INT. HALL. NIGHT

Alex enters the flat. The hall is dark but light comes from the living
room. He moves towards it.

INT. LIVING ROOM. NIGHT

Alex opens the door. Juliet sits with her back to him, while David looks

213

out of the window. Concerned for Juliet, Alex approaches her.

ALEX

Are you all right?

JULIET

Yes, of course. Why wouldn't I be?

Rebuffed, Alex takes in the situation.

ALEX

I don't know. I thought maybe I was –

JULIET

We were just sorting things out.

She and David exchange a glance.

ALEX

Well, you'd better read all about it.

Alex drops the newspapers on the table in front of Juliet.

The headline reads 'TRIPLE CORPSE HORROR'.

DAVID

We already know. All about it.

JULIET

It was on the television.

Alex picks up the papers.

ALEX
(*nervously*)

Of course, but I think you'll find the print medium provides a more lucid and detailed –

JULIET

Oh, shut up, Alex.

DAVID

It wasn't deep enough. I told you it wasn't deep enough, but you wouldn't listen.

ALEX

It doesn't necessarily matter. They don't even know who those people are, and even if they did, they have nothing to connect them with us, nothing at all.

DAVID

I'm glad that you're so certain, Alex. It makes us feel a whole lot better.

ALEX

I beg your pardon?

JULIET

It makes us feel a whole lot better.

ALEX

That's what I thought he said.

INT. ALEX'S ROOM. NIGHT

Alex lies asleep. Slow track towards him.

INT. KITCHEN. DAY. DREAM

McCall and Mitchell are standing in the centre of the kitchen. They say nothing. Mitchell leans down and begins to poke at the slender gap between two floorboards as though trying to get his finger into it. This appears impossible but he manages nevertheless. His finger digs in, while McCall watches. Gradually Mitchell takes a grip of the floorboard. It is nailed down fast and Mitchell strains as he pulls. Eventually the nails fly out and, in a flurry of cracks and splinters, the plank comes away.

McCall and Mitchell look down. In the gap between the rafters, Alex is lying face down and trying to crawl away under the floorboards.

Mitchell grabs Alex's ankle and McCall is now holding a saw.

INT. ALEX'S ROOM. NIGHT

Alex awakens abruptly and in shock. He is sweating. Just as he recovers his composure, he sees a form, almost hidden in the darkness, sitting on the end of his bed.

ALEX

Who the fuck?

He braces himself for a fight and fumbles at the bedside light switch.

JULIET

Sshh. Stop.

Alex leaves the light off.

ALEX

What are you doing here?

Juliet pauses.

JULIET

It's about me and David.

ALEX

The perfect couple, I should say.

JULIET

You mustn't take it so badly.

ALEX

Don't worry about it. I'd do exactly the same, but I don't think I'm his type.

JULIET

Don't you ever stop?

ALEX

No.

Alex slumps back, eyes closed, asleep almost instantly.

Juliet watches him.

INT. LIVING ROOM. DAY

McCall and Mitchell sit opposite Juliet, who is being questioned. They watch her while she studies photographs of Hugo, Tim and Andy intently. Eventually, McCall breaks the silence. Mitchell takes notes continuously.

MCCALL

Take all the time you like, doctor.

JULIET

I'm sorry, I've never seen any of them.

MCCALL

Look again if you like.

Juliet glances at the photographs.

JULIET

No. I haven't seen them.

MCCALL

Do you think you have a good memory for faces?

JULIET

Same as everyone else.

MCCALL

But in your work you must meet lots of different people, every day – new people, new faces. No?

JULIET

Yes.

MCCALL

And what do you recognize, names or faces?

JULIET

Diseases.

MCCALL

Like recognizing criminals by their crimes.

JULIET

I suppose so.

MCCALL

I mean, that's what it's like.

JULIET

Sorry?

MCCALL

And you said you supposed so, but I wasn't offering it for debate.

MITCHELL

Offering it for debate.

MCCALL

It's like recognizing criminals by their crimes.

INT. ALEX'S ROOM. DAY

Alex sits on his bed. Beside him are the copies of the newspaper that he brought home with the headline 'TRIPLE CORPSE HORROR'. He lifts one and tears at the front page.

*[INT. LIVING ROOM. DAY

McCall and Mitchell sit facing David. He is looking at the photographs of Hugo, Tim and Andy (as they were when alive). They are official, mug-shot snaps. David shows no hint of recognition.

DAVID

No, I've never seen them.

MCCALL

You're sure of that.

DAVID

Yes.

MCCALL

That wasn't a question.

MITCHELL

You can tell by the intonation.

MCALL

One other thing. Do you have any tattoos?

DAVID

No.

McCall points at the photograph of Tim.

*Cut from completed film.

MCCALL

Neither does he.

David and McCall both look at the photograph.

A small trickle of plaster and dust falls from the ceiling and lands on McCall's knee. He wipes it off and looks up. David sees but does not look up.]

INT. LIVING ROOM. DAY

McCall and Mitchell sit opposite Alex.

*[
ALEX

Is this being recorded?

MCCALL

This is just an informal discussion. ·

ALEX

Are you recording it?

MCCALL

What does it look like?

ALEX

It looks like he's writing everything down.

MCCALL

That's because he is. Does that upset you?

ALEX

No. Why should it?

MCCALL

Well, then?]

ALEX

I've never seen any of these men before.

MCCALL

Take another look at these two.

*Cut from completed film.

ALEX

I don't know them.

MCCALL

And if I told you their car was parked outside, would that surprise
you?

ALEX

Yes, I suppose so.

*McCall gathers up the photographs and puts them into an inside
pocket.*

Well, is it?

MCCALL

What?

ALEX

Parked outside?

INT. LOFT/LIVING ROOM (FROM ABOVE). DAY

MCCALL

No, not any more. I just wondered if it would surprise you.

INT. LOFT. DAY

David steps back from the hole above the living room. He is puzzled.

INT. LIVING ROOM. DAY

Alex's interrogation continues.

MCCALL

That's it, then.

ALEX

That's all?

MCCALL

Yes. Sorry to waste your time.

ALEX

Oh, no problem. Don't worry.

MCCALL

Just one thing.

ALEX

Yes.

MITCHELL

That watch.

ALEX

What?

MCCALL

Your watch.

MITCHELL

Is it real?

MCCALL

Or a fake?

ALEX

What? Uh, no, no, it's a fake. I picked it up in Thailand. The second hand doesn't sweep, you see.

MCCALL

I see.

Mitchell takes a note of this.

ALEX

Right.

MCCALL

Tell you what. If you do remember seeing any of these guys, maybe you could give me a phone, on this number, any time you like.

He holds out a card for Alex. Alex hesitates and then takes the card.

INT. HALL. NIGHT

The hall is empty but we can hear voices from the living room.

ALEX

I didn't tell them anything. Nothing at all, absolutely nothing.

221

They're plods, that's all they are. If they had anything, anything at all to connect us, any witnesses, any forensic evidence, they'd have whipped it out there and then.

INT. LIVING ROOM. NIGHT

Alex, Juliet and David are in the room.

> DAVID

But they know.

> ALEX

They can know all they like, it won't do them the slightest bit of good –

> DAVID

They know.

> ALEX

They know? So what? They have nothing, there is nothing, to connect us to that bodies stuff.

> DAVID

Except the money.

> JULIET

He's right, Alex. They know.

INT. HALL. NIGHT

The empty hall and closed door as before.

INT. LOFT. NIGHT

The loft is dark but a small amount of light filters in, revealing David's face on the pillow. He is awake. In his hand he holds the Polaroid of Alex. He examines it, then, reaching up, he pins it to a rafter so that Alex's face stares down at him.

There is movement in the bed beside him. It is Juliet, asleep.

INT. ALEX'S ROOM. NIGHT

Alex is also awake. He sits up and reaches out for some clothes.

INT. LOFT. NIGHT

Juliet sleeps, while David slowly extricates himself from the bed.

He lifts the lid of the tank and pulls at a piece of string, on the end of which is the thick yellow plastic bag.

INT. ALEX'S ROOM. NIGHT

Faintly lit by a dimmed lamp, Alex opens the door to the hall.

INT. LOFT. NIGHT

David makes his way to the trapdoor and slowly opens it. The door creaks once and Juliet mutters in her sleep but does not wake.

INT. ALEX'S ROOM. NIGHT

Hearing the creak, Alex freezes in mid-dial, but hears nothing more. He starts to dial again, then stops and replaces the receiver but continues to hold it.

INT. HALL. NIGHT

David drops to the floor with the money.

INT. DAVID'S ROOM. NIGHT

The light is on. David dresses quickly but quietly and pulls a bag from under his bed, into which he puts some clothes, his passport, etc.

INT. ALEX'S ROOM. NIGHT

Alex lifts the receiver again and dials. He stares at a card in his hand. It is the one given to him by McCall.

INT. DAVID'S ROOM. NIGHT

David is now wearing a coat and is finished packing. He glances quickly around his room for the last time, then lifts the two bags and switches off his light.

INT. HALL. NIGHT

As David closes his door behind him he disappears into the darkness of the hall.

Suddenly he is brightly illuminated as the main light goes on.

Juliet stands by the door of the flat, dressed to leave.

JULIET

You forgot to wake me.

INT. ALEX'S ROOM. NIGHT

Alex sits still, listening to David and Juliet. He ignores the message that can be heard coming over the telephone.

WOMAN'S VOICE

This office is closed at present. In the event of an emergency, please contact the duty officer via the switchboard. If you wish to leave a message, please speak clearly after the tone, leaving your name, address and telephone number.

Over this, David and Juliet can be heard from the hall.

JULIET

So let's go.

DAVID

You and me?

INT. HALL. NIGHT

David and Juliet stand as before.

JULIET

Together.

David nods, then steps across the hall, leans down and pulls the telephone cable from its socket in the wall. He calls out to Alex.

DAVID

Hey, Alex, who are you calling at this time of night? Come on out and talk to us.

Alex appears at the door of his room. He is not angry, but wary.
Juliet is not sure what David is playing at.

Well?

Alex says nothing.

Sex lines? Is that it? Triple X-rated interactive fantasy? Old habits
die hard.

ALEX
Yeah, I was phoning your mother.

DAVID
You old devil. Well, anyway, as you can see, we're leaving.

ALEX
So I gathered.

DAVID
Yeah, I'm sorry, but that's the way it is.

ALEX
It's all right. I'll forward your mail.

DAVID
No, really, I am sorry, sorry to be ducking out on you like this. I
hope you won't take it personally.

ALEX
Oh, no, no, no. Don't let it worry you. Not at all. It's probably for
the best.

DAVID
For the best. Exactly. I wouldn't want things to end on a downer.

ALEX
Not at all.

DAVID
I mean, we've had ups and downs, right – good times, bad times?

ALEX
Yeah.

DAVID

But more laughter than tears, I think? Yes. On balance? I mean, remember that time when – oh, we could talk all night, but we have to go. Don't we, Juliet?

JULIET

Yes.

DAVID

And you need your sleep.

ALEX

Yes.

David pauses in thought.

DAVID

No, can't think of anything else that matters.

ALEX

About the mail –

DAVID

It's very kind of you to offer, but –

ALEX

Where do you think you'll go?

DAVID

Where will we go? Where will we go? Juliet?

He turns to her.

JULIET

Eh, I don't know.

DAVID

Oh, don't be so coy, dear. You're going to Rio.

JULIET

What?

DAVID

That's right. You're going to Rio. Rio de Janeiro. On your own. Come on, you should know. You bought the fucking ticket.

David produces Juliet's airline ticket from a pocket and hands it to Alex, who looks at it before putting it in a pocket.

Do you see that? Did you know about it? I'll bet you she didn't tell you about that before she sent you up there. You could have died. What did she say, 'We'll split it together, you and me, fifty fifty'?

He turns to Juliet.

But I bet you didn't say you were going to split on him.

JULIET

It wasn't like that.

DAVID

Don't lie to me. Don't treat me like that.

ALEX

I bought it.

Juliet looks to Alex in surprise. David is momentarily confused.

DAVID

What?

ALEX

I bought the tickets. One for her and one for me. It was my idea.

DAVID

Your idea? Well, that fits. I mean, the two of you, that fits together. I should have seen that long ago.

David picks up his bags and starts walking to the door.

Juliet bars his way. He stops.

David gently shoves past her, but Juliet overtakes him and stands right in front of the door. David stops again.

JULIET

Stop him, Alex. You've got to stop him.

ALEX

Let him go. Let him take it all.

David steps forward, but Juliet is pressed against the door. He drops his holdall and reaches for the door handle. Juliet tries to push him back. They struggle but neither is winning. David relaxes.

DAVID

I'm going.

David pauses for a moment, then hits Juliet once in the face, knocking her to the ground.

David looks at her with disdain, then reaches for the door handle. As he does so he is hit from behind by Alex. Surprised as much as hurt, David stumbles round and touches his cheek. Alex is almost apologetic.

ALEX

You shouldn't have hit her. You can do whatever you like, but you shouldn't have hit her.

David takes a step towards the door again, but Alex launches himself at him, forcing him back, where he trips over Juliet's outstretched leg and drops his case. As Alex and David fight briefly on the floor, Juliet picks up the holdall containing the money and throws it into the kitchen.

David forces Alex off and, pushing past Juliet, he enters the kitchen after the bag.

INT. KITCHEN. NIGHT

David stands holding the bag, but a few feet from him, Alex and Juliet block his exit. David holds out the bag temptingly towards Alex.

DAVID

You want it? You want it?

As Alex lunges at the bag, David shifts and kicks Alex in the groin, but is himself immediately stunned again by being hit in the face with the edge of a toaster held by Juliet.

A brutal and angry fight ensues, mainly between Alex and David, around the kitchen and involving various implements and artefacts in it.

Eventually, just as Alex seems to be gaining the upper hand, David reaches out, pulls a long knife from the wooden holder and plunges it with great force through the upper part of Alex's right lung, just beneath his shoulder, pinning Alex to the wooden floor.

David sits up and reaches for a second knife but, as he does so, a blade is forced through his own throat, appearing at the front. Clutching his throat, David falls to the floor, burbling and bleeding to death.

Juliet surveys the scene with shock. She approaches Alex, who cannot reach his left arm over to the knife in his chest. They look into one another's eyes. Neither she nor Alex speaks.

As Juliet carefully touches the knife in his chest, Alex winces. With his right hand he grasps her ankle. She tries to shake herself free, but Alex holds on. She stops and takes off one of her shoes.

JULIET
You did the right thing, but I can't take you with me.

Holding the toe of her shoe, she hammers the top of the knife two or three times, driving it firmly into the floor. Alex's grip falls away. She then puts her shoe back on and picks up the bag of money.

Juliet leaves the kitchen carrying the case. Alex looks to one side,

where David is breathing his last, and to the other into the hall. In the hall, he can see Juliet reappearing from her room, carrying the holdall of money and another bag. She walks back into the kitchen, kneels down and kisses Alex's forehead. At the same time, she takes the airline ticket from his pocket. She stands again and leaves. She disappears from sight and we hear the main door close.

INT. KITCHEN. NIGHT.

Alex lies alone, with David's body beside him.

INT. KITCHEN. DAY

It is brightly lit now. Policemen's legs swarm around Alex, who blinks as a flashlight fires. He looks out to the hall again, where he sees McCall and Mitchell.

Alex lies back, a faint smile on his face.

INT. KITCHEN. DAY

The handle of the knife fills the screen. Moving slowly, the picture tracks down the blade, past Alex's shoulder and down to the pine floor, then through the floorboard to the tip of the blade on the other side. A drop of blood falls from the tip, a few centimetres, on to a thick pile of banknotes.

INT. AN AIRPORT DEPARTURES HALL. DAY

Scraps of ripped newspaper lie scattered around the holdall. Two of the scraps contains the headline 'TRIPLE CORPSE HORROR'.

INT. DAY. MORGUE

A horizontal strip of face. The eyes unmoving and unblinking. We draw back to reveal David laid out on a mortuary tray.

DAVID
(*voice-over*)

Oh, yes, I believe in friends, I believe we need them, but if, one day, you find you just can't trust them any more, well, what then, what then?

Two attendants in white approach across the mortuary and slide the tray into its slot.

Darkness.

CREDITS

Costume Designer	Kate Carin
Sound Mixer	Colin Nicholson
Sound Editor	Nigel Galt
Casting Director	Sarah Trevis
Make-up Designer	Graham Johnston
Art Director	Zoe MacLeod
Assistant Art Director	Tracey Gallacher
Production Buyer	Karen Wakefield
Art Department Assistant	Iain Macaulay
Story Board Artist	John Amabile
First Assistant Director	Ian Madden
Second Assistant Director	Alison Goring
Third Assistant Director	Stephen Docherty
Floor Runner	Niki Longmuir
Script Supervisor	Anne Coulter
Location Manager	Fran Robertson
Production Accountant	Hilda Booth
Production Coordinator	Yvonne McParland
Production Runner	Saul Metzstein
Prop Master	Gordon Fitzgerald
Standby Props	Pat Harkins
Dressing Props	Stewart Cunningham
Props Driver	Scott Kerry
Focus Puller	Ian Jackson
Loader	Lewis Buchan
Grip	Roy Russel
Boom Operator	Tony Cook
Stills Photographers	Nigel Robertson
	Dominic Turner
Re-Recording Mixers	Brian Saunders
	Ray Merrin
Digital Sound Editor	Paul Conway
Footsteps Editor	Richard Fettes
First Assistant Editor	Anuree de Silva
Second Assistant Editor	Neil Williams
Titles Design	Morag Myerscough
Post Production Supervisor	Steve Barker
Music Supervisor	Gemma Dempsey
Special Make-up Effects	Grant Mason
Special Visual Effects	Tony Steers
Make-up Assistant	Carmel Jackson
Wardrobe Supervisor	John Norster

233

Stunt Arranger	Clive Curtis
Gaffer	Willie Cadden
Best Boy	Mark Ritchie
Electrician	Arthur Donnelly
Genny Operator	Derrick Ritchie
Construction Manager	Colin H. Fraser
Construction Chargehand	Derek Fraser
Standby Carpenters	Brian Adams
	Danny Sumsion
Standby Rigger	Kenny Richards
Standby Stage	Bryan Boyne
Standby Painter	Jim Patrick
Carpenters	Peter Knotts
	Richard Hassall
	John Watts
Painters	Paul Curren
	Sam Curren
Stage	Campbell Atkinson
Scenic Artist	Stuart Clark
Runners	James Stewart
	Mat Bergel
	Eric Smith
	Jamie Spencer
Trainees	Gina Lee
	Kirstin McMahon
	Dianne Jamieson

'Shallow Grave'
Written by Neil Barnes/Paul Daley
Performed by Leftfield
Courtesy of Hard Hands Ltd

'Happy Heart'
Written by James Last/Jackie Rae
Performed by Andy Williams
Published by Donna Music Ltd
Courtesy of Sony Music Entertainment Inc.

'My Baby Just Cares For Me'
Written by G. Kahn/W. Donaldson
Performed by Nina Simone
Published by EMI Music Publishing Ltd
Courtesy of Bethlehem Music

'Release The Dub'
Written by Neil Barnes/Paul Daley
Performed by Leftfield
Courtesy of Hard Hands Ltd

Television Clips

Scotland Today and *Shadowing*
Courtesy of Scottish Television PLC

Lose a Million
Courtesy of Actiontime, Carlton Television and Chris Tarrant
Carlton Music/EMI Music Publishing Ltd

The Wickerman
Courtesy of Lumière Pictures Ltd

Filmed on location in Glasgow and Edinburgh

Shallow Grave is a Film Four International and Glasgow Film Fund
presentation of a Figment Film